Angel's Mother's Boyfriend

Angel's Mother's Boyfriend

JUDY DELTON

Illustrated by Jill Weber

Houghton Mifflin Company
Boston

Library of Congress Cataloging-in-Publication Data

Delton, Judy.
Angel's mother's boyfriend.

Summary: Ten-year-old Angel finds plenty to worry about
when she learns that her mother's new boyfriend is a clown.
[I. Single-parent family — Fiction]
I. Title.
PZ7.D388Ap   1986   [Fic]   85-27054
ISBN 0-395-97913-7

Printed in the United States of America
BP 10 9 8 7 6 5 4 3 2 1

For Kathy Krull,
who says I write like an angel

CONTENTS

ONE

Trouble from Washington

Angel sat on her back steps, thinking. Her mother was just home from a trip to Canada and was humming in the kitchen of their old green house on Kilbourn Avenue. Ever since her mother had come home, Angel had noticed a lightness in her step and a sort of look about her as though she had a secret — a nice secret — something soft and warm hidden down deep where no one else can see. In fact, thought Angel, her mother was acting like a schoolgirl, Angel's age.

Mrs. O'Leary had needed the vacation, Angel

knew. It was her first in twelve years, since the children had been born. As Alyce (her baby sitter and her mother's friend) had said, she needed to get away—from her job, from the children, and from the work of raising a family alone.

But it made Angel nervous having her mother young and happy with a secret. Especially since she, Angel, felt older since her mother had come home. When Alyce had broken her leg and gone to the hospital, Angel was left in charge of the big old house and her small brother, Rags. (His real name was Theodore. Angel's real name was Caroline.) Rags had been in all sorts of trouble and Angel had been responsible for not only his life, but the running of the house and Alyce and her broken bones and her pets and her relatives. It was enough to age anyone, thought Angel soberly. All of these grown-up experiences at only ten made her feel wiser, as well. Old and wise Angel, who had a mother who was getting younger all the time.

If it continued, Angel mused, they could end up the same age! Or, heaven forbid, Angel would grow older than her mother and be taking care of her! In her mind's eye, she saw her mother going off to St. Mary's School, and Angel, poor forgotten Angel, in the thankless role of a mother before her time. Well, she had had enough experience mothering Rags. She could cook meals, she supposed, and wash and iron clothes, and go to work and do the marketing. She pondered briefly what she would call her mother — by her proper name? She caught herself as she was picturing her mother in her Brownie uniform selling cookies. Her mother was right — she did have a "wild imagination."

Angel stood up and stretched and tried to clear her mind of such improbable (impossible, really) happenings. Just because she felt old and her mother looked young did not mean they would really *get* that way! She felt guilty about her imagination. If she really was wise and old, she would know better.

Looking down the street, she saw a familiar red sweat jacket with a red hood.

"Edna!" she called. Edna was walking slowly, kicking an old pop can. She usually didn't bother with things like that. She usually walked briskly, even ran, with her hair flying behind her. Angel knew what was the matter. Edna, who had thought it a lark when Angel's mother went out of town, was not enjoying being in charge herself. Edna had never had to fend for herself before, and while she envied Angel, she was alarmed when her own mother had left her to go on a business trip with her father.

It's funny what a mother does for a house, thought Angel as she watched Edna come down the street. She remembered that when she and Rags were alone, or even with Alyce, the house looked different, the food looked different, the clothes came out of the washer different, and even their very bodies looked different. There was something about Edna's clothes today that didn't seem right. They did not exactly match, and her hair was a different style. It looked like it was the opposite of the way it wanted to grow, like a cowlick forced to turn around, and as a result it stood straight up on her head. Angel remembered that look. It included tying her braids with string or a rubber band instead of crisp hair ribbons and Rags wearing a white T-shirt that had a dingy pink glow to it. There was no doubt, a mother did some mysterious thing to a family. Something you didn't notice till she was gone.

Edna turned in at Angel's garden gate and sat down beside her on the steps. She put her chin in her hands.

"Mabel keeps wanting to comb my hair," sighed Edna. "Like I'm a little kid or something." Mabel was Edna's baby sitter.

"At least you *have* a baby sitter," said Angel wisely. "I had to take care of myself and everything else," and she thought of Rags, who was busy at work on the miniature town he was continually digging under the house. Their mother worried that someday he would dig away the foundation and the house would fall, but so far that hadn't happened.

"And my mother never calls, like your mom did," Edna went on.

"She's probably busy," said Angel. "I mean, it isn't that she doesn't *care* about you..."

Now Angel was taking the role that Edna had taken when Angel's mother was out of town, saying all those things that Edna had said to cheer her only a month before! Life is strange, thought Angel, changing so fast and when you least expect it!

"And Mabel makes me eat this sticky oatmeal in the morning before I'm even awake." Edna made sick noises and hugged her stomach. "And I could be anywhere. She doesn't keep track of me. She doesn't say, 'Be home before dark, Edna,' or 'Is your homework done?' or 'Wear a heavier coat outside, you might catch a cold.' No one even *cares!*" she wailed.

This was an entirely new Edna, thought Angel.

Edna usually was so confident and self-assured. She always took charge in a situation when Angel would just panic or be indecisive.

"*You* can do your own homework and be in before dark yourself and wear the coat you need—you know all that," said Angel.

Edna wiped her eyes. "But how does *she* know that?" said Edna. "If Mabel was babysitting Rachel Fedders, Rachel would be out all night!"

Angel gave that some thought, to be fair to Edna. It was true. Rachel would be the kind of girl to take advantage of a situation. "But you aren't Rachel," she said. "And Mabel isn't sitting for the Fedderses."

Edna just shook her head and frowned. Angel felt like Edna's mother. This older feeling must be what growing up is all about, she thought. "Why don't you stay overnight tonight," said Angel in her new, motherly voice.

Edna blew her nose and said she'd love to, and she went in and called Mabel to tell her. Mrs.

O'Leary made the children a regular supper with salad and meat and potatoes and dessert, and Edna forgot that she felt unloved. She and Angel sat at the dining room table and did their homework. When they went to bed they lay awake for a long time talking, and Angel couldn't help but feel glad that *her* mother was at home where she belonged, cooking dinner and running the house, and that it was Edna's mother, not hers, who was on a business trip. This made her feel a bit guilty and she decided to be extra nice to Edna until her mother returned.

Angel walked Edna home after school the next afternoon. When she came to her own house, she found Alyce there, having a cup of tea with her mother. Angel could hear them talking and laughing about something as she was walking up the back steps, but they stopped when Angel entered.

"Hello, dear!" said her mother in an unnaturally high voice. "Will you get the mail from the box? I forgot when I came in from work."

Her mother seemed to forget a lot of things lately, Angel noted. She put her books on the dining room table and started for the front porch. As she did, she noticed that her mother and Alyce had begun to talk and laugh again. Maybe they were talking about her, she thought. Or about that secret Angel felt sure her mother had.

She reached into the mailbox and took out the phone bill and an ad for a new home delivery pizza house and two other envelopes addressed to her mother in large, firm black handwriting. The handwriting was familiar. These envelopes had been coming in the mail almost every day since her mother had returned from Canada. The return address had no name, just "198 Lyric Lane, Washington, D.C."

Could they be from some government agency? Perhaps her mother hadn't paid her income tax on time. Whatever it was, it must be urgent. The letters were becoming more frequent. Two in one day must mean trouble.

Angel took the mail in to her mother, and again the voices ceased as she drew near.

Her mother looked through the mail and held up the two letters from Washington for Alyce to see.

"This must be serious!" said Alyce in an alarming voice.

Serious! She was right. Her mother was in some kind of trouble.

Angel sighed and went to her room. Just when she thought her responsibilities were over. Just when her mother returned and Alyce left and Angel thought she could relax. Now there was something brand new to worry her. It seemed as if she was never able to be free of some worry. Her mother was trying to be brave, to act as if nothing was the matter, with her laughter and carefree manner, but Angel could see through it all.

When Angel changed her clothes and went downstairs, she noticed that the phone bill and pizza ad were still on the table, but the two letters from Washington were gone. Alyce was gone too, and her mother was in the kitchen starting supper.

"Angel," she called, "would you take Rags for a walk or to the playground while I get supper?

I think he spends too much time under the porch. It doesn't seem healthy."

Angel nodded and called to Rags, who was turning Angel's old tricycle upside down and spinning the pedals.

"Where're we going, Angel?" said Rags.

"To Edna's," said Angel. Rags was glad for any outing.

Edna was in her back yard filling some clay pots with dirt. "Mabel said I could plant tomato seeds in these pots and when they get a foot high, I can plant them outside. I'm going to surprise my mom and dad!"

Angel was glad to notice that Edna was feeling better, because she really wasn't in the mood to hear about all of Mabel's failings. The girls sat down on the steps and Rags played on the swing set.

"There's something the matter with my mom," said Angel. "I think she's in some kind of trouble." Angel told Edna about the letters that kept coming every day with the same handwriting.

"And they're from Washington," added Angel.

"Are they from the White House?" asked Edna. "Or the Capitol, or the Pentagon?"

"Maybe," said Angel. "Probably."'

Edna whistled a long, low whistle. "We'd better do something to help," she said. Edna always liked a problem to solve, especially if it was Angel's.

"What can we do?" said Angel. "We don't even know what the matter is."

"Does your mom cry a lot?" said Edna.

"No, she just acts different since she came home."

The girls sat thinking for a while.

"I suppose the one way we could find out would be to open the letters," said Edna.

Angel was shocked. "You can't open mail that isn't yours," she said. "It's against the law. We would be in trouble in Washington ourselves then!"

"Usually letters from Washington mean you owe money," said Edna wisely. "Like taxes or fines or things."

"Do you think my mom owes money?"

Edna shrugged. "Maybe," she said. "That might worry her."

"What do they do in Washington if you don't pay?"

"They lock you up in jail, " said Edna confidently. "I saw this movie on TV where they just came and took the guy away in handcuffs one night."

Kidnapping! Angel was on the verge of tears. Something must have happened on the trip that her mother had not told them. She only related the good parts, the happy parts. And she brought gifts to pretend nothing was wrong. But her mother had never acted this new way, and she had never received letters from Washington in her life. Angel brought in the mail most of the time, and she knew.

"This guy on TV got letters from Washington, too," said Edna, getting involved in the problem. "And phone calls, too. Does your mom get any phone calls?"

"No," said Angel, alarmed. That was a new

worry. Now Angel would listen all night for the phone to ring, even the doorbell. The kidnappers could come without warning and take her mother away.

"I think," said Edna sensibly, "that you should talk to your mother about it. Ask her what is the matter."

Angel shook her head. "I can't ask her. She's trying to keep us from knowing. She's trying to act brave."

"Well, then, I think you should watch and listen and find out from what she says on the phone, like to Alyce. Then, if we know she is in trouble with the government or the law, we can go on to Plan B."

"Plan B?" said Angel. Edna sounded as though she knew just what to do, almost professional. That was comforting to Angel. She would do as Edna said. At least she'd be taking action. It would feel better to be taking some kind of action.

"Plan B would be to get some money for your mom," said Edna.

15

It sounded simple. "How could we do that?"

Edna sighed. "Well, let's not cross that bridge till we come to it," she said, sounding just like a mother. "We can decide that when we find out the problem is real."

Angel called Rags and said good-bye to Edna. It was time to get started on what must be Plan A, listening and watching.

"I'm glad you don't feel so bad about your mom being gone," said Angel as she was leaving.

"She's coming back this Sunday," said Edna. "I got a letter after school."

Well, that would solve Edna's problem, thought Angel. But it had been only the beginning of Angel's: having her mother come home again.

TWO

Plan B: Money for the Kidnappers

"Angel and Rags," her mother was calling as Angel came down the street. "Supper is ready."

After the children washed their hands and sat down at the table, their mother dropped the silverware on the floor.

"My!" she exclaimed. "How clumsy of me!" Rags scampered over to pick it up, and Angel sighed. "I must be nervous about something," she said with a kind of giggle. Their mother usually did not giggle.

"Have some potatoes, dear, and some rice,"

said Mrs. O'Leary. She put a helping of each on Rags's plate.

"Where is the meat?" said Angel.

"I thought we'd just have leftovers tonight," said Mrs. O'Leary.

Angel looked at the white potatoes on her plate and the white rice beside it. Maybe she was making too much of this, but she was sure they usually had meat and a salad, and sometimes even dessert. Her mother had a faraway look in her eye. She didn't even notice that half their supper was missing!

Rags, innocent that he was, was humming under his breath and eating happily. He had no worries about the lack of iron and protein in his diet and his need for leafy greens.

All of a sudden the phone rang, and Mrs. O'Leary stood up so quickly that she knocked her chair over! "I'll get it," she said, and ran from the table.

"Bang! Crash!" said Rags, waving his fork, enjoying the excitement of silverware and chairs falling with a clatter.

Angel took a notepad out of her blouse pock-et and, with a stub of a pencil she had put there for this purpose, wrote down, "Silverware, chair." Actually, she wouldn't forget to report these clues to Edna, but it would be more offi-cial to have it in writing.

Their mother was gone quite some time. When she came back to the table, she looked mysterious. "That was a call from Washington, D.C.," she said.

This time it was Angel who dropped her sil-verware. Things were happening too fast. Edna had just mentioned phone calls and now here was one! Edna must have ESP! She should be a fortuneteller!

Just when Angel hoped (or feared) that her mother would say more about the caller, there was a knock on the back door and Alyce walked in.

"You two finish up now," said their mother. "I want to talk to Alyce in the living room."

Mrs. O'Leary left her plate of cold food on the table and, taking her coffee cup and one for Alyce, went into the living room. Angel had

trouble hearing them. She wrote "phone call" on her notepad, then crept closer to the living room doorway to listen.

"What?" Alyce was shrieking. "Coming here? He's coming here?"

Angel couldn't hear her mother's reply. Perhaps she was crying. Angel wrote the conversation down quickly on her notepad. Then there was some animated conversation she couldn't get and then louder tones, Alyce again.

"But what about money?" she was saying.

Angel wrote it down. She didn't get Alyce's next sentence, but she heard the last three words: "rob a bank."

"I knew it!" said Angel, putting her notepad back in her pocket. "I knew it," she called to Rags as she ran out of the house and over to Edna's. Rags put down his fork and followed, Angel chattering to him all the way about Plan B.

"Mom is in trouble, Rags. We have to get some money for her to pay off her debts before the men from Washington come and take her away to jail."

Rags began to sob quietly as he ran beside Angel, his short legs trying to keep up with her longer ones. His mother had just returned; he didn't want her to go away again.

When Angel got to Edna's, she told her the whole story—the phone call, the talk about someone from the government coming, and the words "rob a bank."

"It happened just as you said," cried Angel, "only faster."

"Plan B," said Edna grimly. "We have to get enough money together to get your mom out of this trouble, and we have to do it before she robs a bank."

Rags by now was distracted by Edna's dog, who brought a stick to him to throw for a game of fetch. Rags threw it, and the dog brought it back and dropped it on Rags's lap.

"Good boy!" said Rags, patting the dog's head. "Edna," he added, "your dog is dirty. He needs a bath."

"He's going to the Poodle Parlor when my mom gets home," said Edna.

The word "mom" brought back Rags's worries about his own mother and the trouble she was in.

"Will Mom go away again?" he whimpered to Angel.

"Unless we think of a way to help," she said. "Think, Rags. Think of a way to earn money to get her out of trouble."

Rags reached into his pocket and took out a dime and three pennies.

Angel shook her head. "We need a *lot* of money, Rags. The government doesn't want thirteen cents."

"How much do you think she owes?" asked Edna.

"A lot," said Angel. "It must be a lot."

"How much is a lot?" said Rags.

"I don't know. Probably a million dollars," said Angel.

Rags let out a low whistle under his breath which he'd learned from Angel. "Can we get a million dollars, Angel?"

"Of course not," said Angel impatiently.

Rags looked tearful again. Angel was usually able to solve all their problems.

"Maybe the government would take a down payment," said Edna thoughtfully. "I mean, if we had some money to give him when the man comes, we could give him an IOU for the rest."

That made sense to Angel. The main thing was to waylay the kidnapper and keep their mother safe.

"I don't have even a little money," said Angel, thinking of the fine the children had incurred when Rags wrote in wet cement on the school sidewalk. It seemed as if there was always something to pay off, something to use up her allowance every week.

"Well, we'll get it like everyone else does," said Edna. "We'll earn it."

"How?" said Angel and Rags together.

"Well, let's think," said Edna.

Edna's dog came and lay his head in Rags's lap.

"Good boy," said Rags. "It's good you're getting a bath soon."

"That's it!" said Edna. "I know how we can earn money! We can open a dog laundry! I know lots of people who don't like to give their dogs baths, and lots of older ladies can't get their dogs into a tub! And it costs ten dollars at the Poodle Parlor. If we did it for *five,* we'd only have to do ten dogs to have fifty dollars! If we did twenty, we'd have *one hundred!* That would surely be enough for a down payment."

Rags jumped up and down. "Let's do it!" he said without thinking. Angel got cross when she thought about how immature Rags was. He was such a baby. He never planned things or thought of what the consequences would be. He was fickle. He was lucky to have Angel to do the thinking for both of them.

"It does seem like fast money, and something we may be equipped to do," said Angel thoughtfully.

"Of course it is," said Edna. "Anyone can wash a dog! And if we charged six dollars instead of five, we would only have to launder"—

here Edna paused to do some arithmetic in the air — "about sixteen and a half dogs to earn one hundred dollars."

Rags laughed at the thought of a half of a dog in the laundry tub. Angel agreed that six dollars was reasonable and that sixteen dogs should not be too many to wash in one day. They would have to work fast, before the man came from Washington.

"Now," said Edna. "Where will we do it?"

"My mom goes to work early tomorrow morning," said Angel, "and it's Saturday. That's a good day for business. We can use our laundry tubs."

"We'd better put signs up tonight," said Edna. "There isn't a moment to lose."

Edna went into the house and got some crayons and pencils and paper and thumbtacks. By the time they had finished the signs and tacked them onto trees around town, it was growing dark.

"I'll be over first thing in the morning," called Edna as they parted.

THREE

The Dog Laundry

When Angel and Rags got home, Angel was surprised to see that their mother was not looking for them. Usually, whenever it got the least bit dark, Mrs. O'Leary would look up and down the streets nervously. Now she was in the house, at the dining room table, writing a letter. She looked up at them when they came in, as if she was surprised they were there.

"Dear me, I thought you two were in bed!" she said. "Isn't it past your bedtime?"

It was not like their mother to forget what

time it was, thought Angel, or to let her children roam the streets at night like ordinary hoodlums. Or orphans. No, their mother was distracted by those letters. The one she was writing at this moment was probably a plea to spare her life.

When Angel got to her room, she made a sign to put over the door (after her mother had gone to work) so that people would know about the laundry location. It read: DOG LAUNDRY HERE. DOGS WASHED: $6 EACH.

In the morning, Angel heard her mother call upstairs that breakfast was ready and that she was leaving for work. Angel jumped out of bed and into her jeans and T-shirt (suitable dog-washing clothes, she thought) and ran down-stairs into the dining room. Before she was through with breakfast, Edna was at the door.

When Angel opened the door to let her in, she couldn't believe her eyes. There, behind Edna, was a long line of dog owners with their dogs on leashes — red, blue, and yellow leashes — and some on just a piece of rope. There were poodles, beagles, cocker spaniels, Irish setters; some sitting, some standing, some barking, some whining, but all of them very, very dirty. And all of them waiting for the laundry to open.

Edna slid in through a small space in the doorway and said, "We'd better get started!"

"Maybe we overadvertised!" said Angel, feeling nervous about this unauthorized business she had opened in her mother's house.

"Naw," said Edna confidently. "We need all the business we can get. I went door to door last night after you left and got lots of people signed up from my own neighborhood."

That explained the long line. Angel ran upstairs and woke Rags up, gave him a banana to eat for breakfast, and helped him get his dog-washing clothes on quickly. "We have lots of work to do!" she told him, tying his tennis shoes.

"Dogs!" shouted Rags, looking out his window. "Look at all the dogs!"

"We have to wash them, Rags. They aren't here to play, you know," Angel reminded him.

When Angel and Rags got downstairs, Edna had let in the first customer, who was chattering away about Ralph's likes and dislikes in the bath. "The water should be warm, but not too warm ..." Ralph was chasing one of the spaniels who was also in line.

Edna took Angel aside for a minute and said, "We need a waiting room for the people in line. We can't just leave them outside."

Angel thought for a minute and decided that the living room would be the logical place, since there were chairs and a couch to sit on.

"You start to wash Ralph, and I'll show the people the waiting room," she said, trying not to think of what would happen if her mother came home from work early. Then she thought of something else. "What about the owners?" she asked. "When we're washing their dogs, should they help us in the basement?"

"Definitely not," said Edna. "I remember when my mom used to take me to the doctor, and the nurse wouldn't let my mom in the examining room with me."

Angel wondered what that had to do with a dog laundry, but she didn't say so.

"Parents interfere," Edna went on, "just like a dog owner would interfere."

So that was it. Edna was right. Owners *would* interfere. They would have to wait in the living room with the others, just as at the Poodle Parlor.

Angel went to the door and said, "Please follow me to the waiting room," to the people in line and also to Ralph's master. When they were seated, Angel found copies of her mother's magazine, *Working Woman,* and one of Alyce's *Sew Easy* magazines and handed them out.

The dogs were pulling on their leashes and sniffing each other and the furniture. The small dogs sat on their owners' laps, but the large ones leaned against the lamps, making them sway precariously.

When Angel got downstairs, she found that Edna and Rags were having trouble getting Ralph into the laundry tub. He stood with his four feet in the water, but all the rest of him was out. Rags was trying to squeeze him together like an accordion, but nothing he did made the dog any smaller.

"We should have thought of this," wailed Angel. "I should have planned for this."

"No problem," said Edna cheerfully. "We'll wash him in your bathtub upstairs. That will be easier anyway because there's a shower — we can rinse the soap off easier. And the tub is lower."

"I have an idea!" said Angel. "We could wash the small dogs down here and the big dogs upstairs!"

"I'll do the small ones, and Rags can help you with the big ones," said Edna. "Then we'll switch, and I'll come upstairs."

Angel took Ralph, who only had wet feet, and led him upstairs, where she had to pass Ralph's owner.

"Through already?" said the owner, putting down *Working Woman*.

"No, no," said Angel. "Don't get up. We just need a larger tub, that's all." The owner frowned, but Angel was already upstairs filling the tub, and Rags was hoisting Ralph in. (Downstairs, Edna was soliciting a small dog from the crowd. Most of the dogs, it appeared, were very large. Edna supposed that owners of small dogs washed their dogs themselves.)

Angel put a capful of bubble bath in the water, and Rags began to scrub Ralph with a bar of soap.

"I think we should use detergent," said Angel, noticing how dirty Ralph was. She reached under the bathroom sink and found Tidal Wave and poured some of it into the water. She took the scrub brush that was next to the detergent and scrubbed Ralph's ears.

Rags scrubbed his back, and Ralph appeared to like it. It wasn't until he got to Ralph's neck that Ralph decided he'd had enough. He began to whine.

All of a sudden, Ralph gave a big lunge and leapt from the tub, full of bubbles.

"Get him!" shouted Angel.

Rags sped down the stairs after Ralph, who was already in the living room, shaking off the bubbles.

The owner handed Rags six dollars when he came into the room, put on Ralph's leash, and left.

"He isn't done!" called Rags.

Angel came into the living room and said, "Aw, it's all right, Rags, he was pretty clean."

"But he wasn't rinsed," said Rags.

"Well, he looked clean," Angel assured him. "Let's get the next dog." Angel was surprised at what hard work it was to bathe a big dog. She felt worn out already, trying to keep Ralph in the tub and wash him at the same time.

The next dog in line was a sheepdog named Snooks. Angel frowned. His hair was very, very long. And he had a lot of it.

Snooks jumped right into the tub with no help. "Good dog!" shouted Rags, beginning to scrub him. Angel scrubbed one end and Rags the other, but the more they scrubbed, the more they noticed that Snooks was barely wet, his hair was so heavy.

"Let's turn the shower on, Angel," shouted Rags.

Rags was right, the shower did help. Snooks got wet a bit faster.

Just as they were getting Snooks good and

soapy, Edna stuck her head into the bathroom. She was holding a shivering black poodle.

"Where are the towels?" she said.

"Right here," said Angel. "In the linen closet."

Edna took a large pink one and rubbed the poodle. "What we need," she said, "is a dryer. Have you got one?"

Angel ran into her mother's room and found her hair dryer.

"That isn't too good," said Edna doubtfully. "We could use a big one like they have at the hairdresser's."

Angel felt cross. What did she think they were running, a real business? They were lucky to have *any* hair dryer.

"But it will do," added Edna, sensing Angel's impatience.

She plugged in the hair dryer and soon the poodle stopped shivering and was fluffy and dry.

"It'll take forever to do that sheepdog," said Edna doubtfully.

She was right. After Angel and Rags finished

his bath, they dried and dried him with towels, then they dried and dried him with the hair dryer. Angel hated to admit it, but Edna was right about the hair dryer. They needed a bigger one. Edna was usually right. She knew about a lot of things.

"We are going to have piles and piles of money!" said Rags, showing how high the piles would be with his clean hand. Angel was loading an Airedale into the tub. "Piles and piles!" he repeated, scrubbing the Airedale's ears.

Edna knocked on the door again.

"Have you got any spray perfume?" she asked. "I think it's good for business if the dogs smell good after their bath. They do that at the Poodle Parlor, you know."

Angel went back into her mother's room. "Some of this is expensive stuff," she said.

"It's deductible," said Edna. "You know, this is a business. Your mom can deduct it from her income tax."'

"Really?" said Angel, watching Edna take a bottle of Evening in Madrid and test it. Angel didn't want to think about taxes. Taxes may have been what started this whole thing.

Edna nodded. "This will do fine," she said. She sprayed some on the schnauzer she was holding. He sneezed. "I've done five dogs already," she said proudly as she left. "How many have you and Rags washed?"

"Three," said Rags, holding up three extremely clean fingers.

"The small dogs are almost done," called

Edna as she went down the stairs. "I'll come and help you when I'm through."

Angel looked downstairs. As Edna had said, there were only large dogs left. One was a Saint Bernard.

They dried the Airedale and took him down to his owner in the living room. Then they took the Saint Bernard upstairs.

Rags stared at the Saint Bernard. "He's bigger than I am!" he shouted. "I could ride on his back!" The Saint Bernard wagged his tail. He was drooling.

"Edna," called Angel, "I think we're going to need help now."

Edna finished the terrier she was doing and came upstairs and the three of them tried and tried to get the Saint Bernard into the tub. He refused to budge. He lay down on the bathroom floor and put his huge head on his paws. The three children sat down and looked at him.

"What are we going to do?" cried Angel.

"Let's not panic," said Edna calmly. "We'll think of something."

"We could give him a sponge bath, like Mom gives me sometimes," said Rags.

"Rags is right, you know," said Edna. "We may have to give him a sponge bath."

The Saint Bernard looked like a mountain, lying on the bathroom floor.

Rags had already taken a washcloth and wet it and soaped it and was scrubbing at one of the dog's large feet. "Boy!" said Rags, "You have the biggest feet I ever saw!"

"I'll run a pail of warm water," said Angel, "and we'll do the best we can."

When Angel turned the water tap on, she said, "Guess what? All the warm water is gone."

"Do you have any cold water detergent?" demanded Edna. "My mother has some soap you can use with cold water and it gets things just as clean."

Angel looked doubtful, but she ran down to the basement and found a box that said "For cold water washing" on the side. That was what they had — cold water.

She brought it up and put some in a pail and ran the water over it. It sudsed up, and Edna said, "See? We don't need hot water at all!"

It took the three of them more than half an hour to wash the Saint Bernard, and when they dried him with the towel, some dirt still came off. Rags tried to comb his hair and Edna sprayed some Evening in Madrid on his neck and Angel tied one of her blue hair ribbons on his collar.

"He should have a little extra, because he didn't have a real bath," said Edna sensibly.

By three o'clock in the afternoon, all of the dogs were finished. Angel looked in the living room and didn't see a single dog. She threw herself on her bed, wishing she could take a nap. But the house was a mess, and all the signs had to be taken down from the trees.

Edna took the sign off the door and told Angel and Rags about one lady who had come back to complain that her dog had run out into the garden and rolled in the dirt just after Edna finished washing him.

"What did you do?" said Angel.

"I washed him over again," said Edna, "for free. You have to do that, my dad says, if you have a business. You always have to please the customer."

"You always have to please the customer," said Rags over and over, like a chant. "What's a customer, Edna?"

"Someone you do business with," she said.

"Let's eat lunch," said Angel. "I'm starving."

The children went down to the kitchen and made peanut butter sandwiches. They still felt hungry, so they took a frozen chocolate cake from the freezer and ate it.

Then Rags said, "Let's count our money!"

Rags piled up all the nickels and dimes and quarters into stacks, and Edna and Angel put the dollar bills into piles. Then they counted it.

"One hundred and twenty dollars!" shouted

Angel. "That's more than enough for a down payment!"

Angel picked up twenty dollars and gave it to Edna. "This is for you, Edna. You earned it."

Edna said she liked to wash dogs and didn't want any pay. Angel insisted she take it.

"Maybe we should do this every weekend!" said Edna. "I mean, really go into the dog laundry business."

Angel wasn't sure about that. She thought of how much soap and water and perfume they used. And all the towels that would have to be washed.

"Of course, we probably would need a license if we had a real business," said Edna practically. "It might get too complicated."

Edna helped Angel and Rags clean up the house and scrub the bathtub and sweep the dog hair off the floor and rugs and furniture. Then they went out and took the signs down from all the trees.

Angel put the money for the government in

an envelope marked "Kidnappers" on the front, and said thank you and good-bye to Edna. As she started off for her own house, Rags called out, "Edna! We didn't give *your* dog a bath!"

Edna said he would have to wait till next time — or go to the Poodle Parlor.

Angel was exhausted. She lay down on her bed and waited for her mother to come home from work. She wondered when it would be good to give her the money. Or maybe she should wait and give it to the kidnappers themselves when they came to the door. While she was trying to decide, she fell asleep.

FOUR

Plan C: A Hide-out

While Angel was napping, she dreamed that on a dark and stormy night, amid thunder and bolts of lightning, a government truck drove up to the O'Learys' back door (the truck looked like a post office mail truck). Three men in trench coats (one of the men with a patch over one eye) got out and began to look for Angel's mother and for Angel and Rags. Angel recognized them and took her mother and Rags out the side door and hid the three of them under the porch, behind the latticework, where Rags had built his dirt city.

Somehow the men found them and crawled in after them and chased them wildly up and down the streets of Rags's dirt city, which by then had turned into a city the size of Milwaukee. She and Rags finally managed to evade the men, but Angel's mother was captured.

Angel woke up and rubbed her eyes. Her mother must be home from work, she thought; she heard her voice downstairs on the phone. Angel walked down the stairs with the taste of the kidnapping dream still fresh in her mind.

Mrs. O'Leary sat at the phone, a letter in her hand. "... and he's coming here from Washington, *next week!*" she was saying to someone, probably Alyce, on the other end.

Angel ran out the back door before her mother could see her.

Next week! Things were happening too fast. It was one thing to imagine the kidnapper coming and making sure they had enough money to pay him off, but it was another thing to hear her mother *say* so into the phone so positively.

There seemed to be no doubt at all now that this terrible thing was going to happen.

Before Angel knew where she was going, she found herself at Edna's back door. Mabel answered the door with a pie pan in her hand.

Edna slipped out the screen door with a piece of cherry pie for herself and one for Angel. Besides the sticky oatmeal Mabel made, it appeared she made some good things as well. Edna would probably have gained a lot of weight if her parents were going to be gone much longer.

"Guess what!" said Angel, once they were alone on the back porch. "The kidnapper is coming from Washington next week!"

Edna frowned. "Well, we've got the money," she said.

"But I just had this dream," said Angel, taking a bite of pie, "that the kidnappers chased us. All over. It was awful. They looked like bandits. Rags and I got away, but they got my mom!" Angel stopped to take another bite of pie. "They could take us all captive, Edna! I mean, maybe the money isn't enough. They might want to lock us up!"

"Plan C," said Edna thoughtfully.

Angel didn't know about a Plan C. "What is Plan C?" she said.

"A hide-out," she said. "You've got to find a hide-out."

"Hide-outs are for criminals," said Angel.

"Hide-outs are for anyone who does not want to be found."

That sounded sensible to Angel. She surely did not want to be found. Before Angel could ask "Where?" Edna went on.

"Think of all the hide-outs you know about," she said, eating the last bite of her cherry pie.

Angel thought. "A cave. An abandoned mine shaft."

Edna shook her head. "There are no caves or mine shafts here," she said.

"An old warehouse?" said Angel. "Or a cabin in the woods?"

48

Edna shook her head. "Those are hide-outs in movies. We need one right near here. We have to set it up tonight."

Angel didn't have to ask why. She knew if she wanted Edna's help it must be tonight. Tomorrow her parents would be home.

"I have it!" said Edna. You can hide out in my basement!"

"But your mom and dad are coming home," said Angel. "How can we explain it to them?"

"We won't," said Edna. "We have that outside door to the basement. It goes right down to that old coal bin that's just a storeroom now. No one ever goes there."

Angel began to feel excited. She pictured her mother in a state of panic at the kidnappers' arrival. Just when she was desperately wondering how to save their lives, Angel would take her arm (it would be midnight) and lead her by moonlight the few blocks to safety. There they would have their own hide-out with a private entrance! They could creep undetected to the small windowless room where no one could ever find them, not even the Nazis. (Why in the world did Angel think of the Nazis? She gave a shiver. There were no Nazis. Kidnappers were enough. Why was her imagination giving her more trouble than necessary?)

"You could sneak right in whenever you have to, and we won't even hear you," said Edna, getting excited at the prospect of having Angel living in secret in her basement. She found herself eager for the kidnappers to arrive! She hoped (guiltily) that they did not change their mind at the last minute, and that Angel had heard their time of arrival correctly. "Next week" sounded a bit general.

"Didn't she say what *day* next week?" said Edna.

Angel shook her head. Their own little cozy room was intriguing Angel, too. She wanted to go there tonight!

"Do we need a key?" said Angel.

"No, it's just got a latch on the door you lift up," said Edna. "I'll show you."

The girls ran around to the side yard. Edna lifted up a trap door to reveal a set of secret steps going down to a secret door. It was the ideal hide-out! Edna lifted the latch and pushed the door open, and the girls stepped into a room filled with old trunks and books and shelves full of dusty dishes and tools.

"It's spooky!" said Angel.

"Well, you can't have a fancy hide-out," said Edna, a bit hurt by Angel's response.

"It's . . . *nice!*" said Angel quickly. "I just meant it was a little, ah, dusty."

"Hide-outs are all dusty," said Edna. "I never saw a clean hide-out."

Angel nodded. Edna, like Angel, had probably never seen *any* hide-out. But she didn't say so.

"This is very nice of you," said Angel warmly. "Do you think Mabel heard us?"

Edna shook her head. "Nobody can hear you down here. It's like a tomb."

The girls stood still and listened. It was quiet. Angel noticed that the walls were very old and thick. There couldn't be a better hide-out if one was made to order! It was ideal.

The girls closed the door quietly and went up the steps, closing the trap door after them.

"Now," said Edna, "we have to get supplies."

Angel was impressed with Edna's organization. If it had been up to her, she never would have thought of supplies.

"First of all, you'll need water," said Edna. "And canned food."

"And a can opener," said Angel, glad to make some contribution.

"Now, for a bathroom, what you have to do is after everyone is asleep, you sneak out of the coal bin and there's a little bathroom over in the corner of the basement by the laundry. It's just a toilet and washbowl, but you won't need to take a bath while you're hiding out. You shouldn't be here *that* long."

"The kidnappers will probably leave when they can't find us," said Angel in agreement. "And if they come back, we'll just run over here again, real fast!"

"Of course," said Edna, "they may camp out in your house — or hang around to see if you come back. I think we should take in enough supplies to last a while. Let's get some things from my house and some from yours so no one will be suspicious."

The girls went in the back door of Edna's house, and, sure enough, Mabel didn't mention a word about hearing a noise in the basement. When she went into the living room to watch TV, Edna said, "Quick! Go in the pantry!"

Edna began to take cans off the pantry shelves and put them into a brown grocery bag.

"Do you like carrots?" demanded Edna.

"I do," she said, and Edna put a can in the bag. "But Rags doesn't. He hates them."

Edna took the carrots out. "It has to be something you all like," she said. "How about beets?"

Angel nodded. "We all like beets," she said.

Edna put in salt and ketchup and a can of soup.

"We can't put in things that have to be

cooked," said Angel, "or heated. We haven't got a stove."

"Maybe we could hook up that old hot plate in the basement," said Edna thoughtfully. "No," she said, changing her mind. "Then the smell of food cooking would make my mom suspicious."

She took out the soup and put in a can of sardines. Then she added a package of paper napkins and three knives, forks, and spoons, including a serving spoon.

"I think we should use paper plates," said Angel, "so we don't have to make any noise washing dishes."

"Good idea," said Edna. The girls crept out the back door and back to the cellar and arranged the provisions on a shelf. Angel cleared off an old chair and arranged a few pieces of furniture in a homey grouping.

"You can sleep on those old blankets in the corner," said Edna.

"I'll bring some pillows from home," said Angel.

The girls ran up the stairs and over to the O'Learys' house. Angel's mother was still on the phone, and the letter was on the table.

"Quick!" said Angel. "You get paper plates and stuff from the pantry and I'll run upstairs and get towels and washcloths. And some pillows."

The girls gathered the items and put them into bags, and Angel ran out the front door and in the back to avoid her mother's eyes. "I got a bar of soap and some shampoo and an old tablecloth," said Angel.

"I put in some candles and matches," whispered Edna. "In case the electricity goes off."

"Why would it go off?" asked Angel.

Edna thought for a minute. "It could," she said. "If there was a tornado or something."

The girls were just leaving the house when Mrs. O'Leary hung up the phone.

"Quick!" said Angel. "Run!"

"Angel," called her mother from the back steps. "It's time to come in, dear."

"I'll be home in a few minutes," called Angel from down the street.

The girls stocked the rest of the items in the hide-out, and Edna said, "I'll sneak downstairs tomorrow night after my parents are asleep to see if you're there! And to bring you any emergency supplies."

Angel shuddered. The hide-out didn't seem as inviting as it had earlier in the evening. She felt so tired from the day's events that she longed for her own bed, not a pile of old blankets on a cement floor.

She said good-bye to Edna and ran home. It was bedtime already and her mother, with all her telephoning, seemed to have forgotten that they had not had supper!

FIVE

A New Problem

Angel tumbled into bed. She was so tired that she fell asleep right away. In the morning she and Rags got dressed and came downstairs. Margaret Toomer, who lived across the street, was sitting at the table with their mother, drinking coffee.

"Well, if there's anything I can do to help you out ..." Margaret was saying. "I have an extra bedroom — Angel and Rags could come stay with me ..."

Angel sat on the bottom step and pulled Rags down beside her. Maybe it was time to admit that they knew about the kidnappers. Their mother herself must be worrying about where to escape to; even Margaret was offering a room. Angel supposed she'd better relieve her mother's mind and tell her about the fine arrangements that were already made.

"I think we'll be just fine," their mother was saying. (Bravely, Angel thought.) "I'm really looking forward to it, you know."

Oh, no! Their mother was pretending it was *fun!* She mustn't know how dangerous kidnappers from Washington could be!

Angel ran to her mother and threw her arms around her neck.

"We have some money! We have a hide-out! You don't have to pretend anymore."

Angel began to sob. Rags began to cry, too.

"We know about the men from Washington," Angel cried, "and we have a place to hide. With provisions."

"And we have money," said Rags. "Now they won't take you away."

"Men from Washington? Take me away?" echoed Mrs. O'Leary.

A letter from Washington was still on the table and Angel pointed to it. "It's all right to tell us," she insisted. "We're old enough to know and to help."

"But there isn't any trouble," said their mother. Even now, when the cat was out of the bag, their mother still was trying to protect her children from the truth.

Angel explained about the government letters that they had seen and about overhearing the conversation with Alyce about money and robbing a bank. And the men arriving "next week."

Their mother suddenly got a look on her face which was not alarming, as Angel had feared. No, it had the edges of a smile about it, instead!

"You mean you...Did you think...Oh my goodness. How could I have misled...The letters weren't from the government...I knew I should have explained, but every time I started to, something came up, some interruption..."

"Explain what?" said Angel, who was beginning to feel as if she'd been tricked or been made the butt of a bad joke.

"About Rudy, the nice man I met in Canada," said their mother. "He lives in Washington, D.C., and he was traveling because he was between jobs and had always wanted to go to Toronto."

Angel felt a flood of relief in her stomach when she realized that her mother was not in danger, but at the same time she felt hurt and foolish for jumping to such conclusions. It was her wild imagination again. Her mother always warned her about her imagination. It seemed to play tricks on her.

Mrs. O'Leary put her arms around Angel and hugged her tightly and kept apologizing. Rags had lost interest in the conversation and was shooting Angel's ponytail holders at an imaginary target across the room.

Margaret Toomer looked confused and said, "Well, I was just on my way to church. I will call you . . . later . . ." and left.

"But you told Alyce some man was coming, and she said you had to rob a bank," said Angel, wiping her eyes with a tissue her mother had given her.

"It's Rudy!" said their mother. "He wants to come and see me! And of course he doesn't have much money because he's out of work right now, and Alyce said, 'What will he do for money, rob a bank?' and I told her of course not."

That's what Angel got for listening to bits and pieces of disjointed conversations! And letting her mind leap to wild conclusions. Now she was embarrassed. How would she explain this to Edna? And what about the wonderful, well-stocked hide-out?

Her mother was going on about Rudy and what fun he was and how he had taken her and Angel's Aunt Beth out disco dancing and then to a French restaurant in Toronto and how well she and Rags would like him when he came and what fine letters he wrote.

"He has a marvelous sense of humor!" she concluded, as she stood up and opened the letter in her hand. She began to read it, and a smile came over her face. Then she laughed out loud and said, "Listen to this, Angel," and read her a paragraph about something that had happened to his car. "And then the steering wheel came off in my hands," she read, "and I said, 'Does anyone have a screwdriver?'"

Angel didn't think that was very funny. In the first place, it was dangerous to have a steering wheel come off — her mother wouldn't laugh if it had been *her* steering wheel, or if Angel's bicycle handlebars came off while she was riding and she came home and said, "Look, the handlebars came off, anyone have a screwdriver?"

But by this time her mother was walking to the kitchen, enjoying the letter, and forgetting all about poor little Angel, whose feelings were being cast aside. In fact, both she and Rags seemed to be insignificant lately. Her mother had new things on her mind. New memories, a new person, new jokes, led to a distracted mind. Ordinary things, like her family, were taking a back seat. Angel felt as though her mother hardly saw her around the house anymore. It was like being invisible.

"Are the men coming? Are they coming, Angel? To take Mom away?" whined Rags, who was now tying Angel's hair ribbons around his ankles.

"No," said Angel, taking the ribbons away from Rags, "there are no men from Washington. The letters are from a friend. Didn't you hear Mom tell us?"

"Then we have extra money, Angel! Everything is better, and we have extra money!"

Everything *should* be better, thought Angel. Their mother was not in trouble, and they didn't owe anyone money, and they had an extra hundred dollars to boot. Things definitely sounded better.

Then why did Angel feel worse? She felt lonely and afraid and unloved. And she felt disappointed that all of the rescue plans were dashed.

If her mother had been in trouble, at least they could eventually have earned enough money and gotten out of the trouble, and things would have been normal again. But a new friend, Angel realized suddenly, could change their whole lives. A new friend (especially a man) could mean their mother would be busy every evening, with no time to read stories to Rags (poor Rags!) or play cards with Angel. And if they did do things together, she would be so distracted that she'd do things like drop silverware and knock over chairs. Angel was sure she would forget whose turn it was at Scrabble and put down misspelled words that weren't legal.

The whole thing left an unsettled feeling in Angel's stomach, like the day before a dentist appointment or when there was a substitute teacher at school — you never knew what could happen. What was the matter with having children for friends? Or Alyce? What in the world was the matter with Alyce? Mothers didn't need a lot of friends. Mothers had families.

Angel thought of the mothers she knew. She couldn't remember any of them having friends. They did things with their children.

Angel had come downstairs hours ago with a small problem that she thought was a big problem. Now she walked out of the dining room with a big problem that was *really* a big problem. Her mother had a boyfriend.

"Angel!" called her mother from the kitchen. "The water in the kitchen sink won't go down the drain," she said. "What do you suppose is wrong?"

Before Angel could answer, they heard screams coming from the bathroom upstairs. Rags opened the door, and the water ran out into the hall and slowly down the stairs.

"The toilet ran over!" said Rags, running out into the hall behind the water.

Angel forgot her other problems and helped her mother put Dran-o down the sink and use the plunger in the toilet.

"It doesn't seem to help," said Mrs. O'Leary, surveying the work with her hands on her hips.

"Maybe we have to wait longer," said Angel, reading the directions on the Dran-o can.

Angel and Rags and their mother waited. They waited for ten minutes, then twenty minutes, but still there was no *gurgle, gurgle, splash* that meant water was running down the drain freely. Instead it just stood there, in a dark, greasy puddle.

"We don't need water anyway," said Rags out of the silence.

"Of course we need water," said Angel impatiently.

"Well, we have water," said their mother, turning on the tap lightly. "We just have nowhere to drain it once we have it. I'll have to call the plumber," she went on, after waiting a few more minutes for the water to drain. "It's a Sunday, so it will probably cost more."

"It's probably a grease build-up," said Angel, repeating something she had heard on a TV commercial. No, she remembered, that was on walls or floors. Or was that *wax* build-up? Oh, well, the main thing was that if it could happen to floors and walls, it could happen to pipes. From that greasy dishwater that stood in the sink this minute, for instance. When the plumber saw that, he would say, "Here is our problem." Life was nothing *but* problems, thought Angel. No time just to read a book with an uncluttered mind or without a worry tugging at her stomach.

Mrs. O'Leary leafed through the Yellow Pages and read out loud, "We open your drains twenty-four hours a day."

"That's what we want," chirped Rags. He began to hum, "Open our drains, before it rains..."

Mrs. O'Leary smiled at Rags. She often said his ability to make up rhymes on the spot showed talent, so Rags did it whenever he had the opportunity.

"Twenty-four hours, end of the showers..." he went on, now that he had his mother's attention.

Angel handed her mother the phone impatiently. "Call!" she said.

Their mother called, and the man said he would be out in fifteen minutes. When he arrived, he came into the house dragging long coils of metal, and Rags jumped up and down with excitement.

The plumber checked all the drains carefully. Then he went into the basement and checked carefully. Then he took his equipment into the basement and worked at something noisy for a long time.

When he came upstairs, he held out his hand, which was full of something that he had taken out of the sewer pipe. It didn't look like grease. It looked like — could it be? — *dog hair!* It was gray and black and brown, and it was definitely dog hair. Angel recognized the Saint Bernard's.

"You have a dog?" said the man, an unlit cigarette dangling from his lower lip.

"No," said Mrs. O'Leary quickly. "We have never had a dog."

"Bubba!" said Rags. "Bubba lived here." Bubba was Alyce's dog, who had come with her when she baby-sat for the children just a few weeks earlier.

"Did you bathe him a lot?" the man went on.

Rags shook his head. "He didn't have any bath."

Angel realized that she could no longer let sleeping dogs lie. They had to tell their mother about the dog laundry.

"It's our fault," cried Angel. "We gave a dog a bath yesterday."

"Lots of dogs," said Rags. "Piles and piles of dogs!" Rags spread his arms to encompass all the imaginary dogs he was describing.

Mrs. O'Leary looked at them in surprise.

"We wanted to earn money to help you with the . . . trouble," Angel cried. "It seemed like a good idea."

The plumber was packing up his coils. "You shouldn't have any more trouble," he said.

Angel wished she could believe him. She doubted that they wouldn't have any more

71

trouble; in fact, she was sure this was just the beginning.

"That will be fifty-two dollars," said the plumber, doing some arithmetic on the side of his tool box. "Sundays are double time."

"Wait!" shouted Angel. She ran and got the kidnapper's envelope. She counted out exactly fifty-two dollars and handed it to the man while their mother watched in amazement. "It was our fault," said Angel.

The man got into his truck and drove off, and Angel's mother said, "Let's talk about all of this later," and she went to her room to lie down.

Angel got sponges and wiped up the water in the hallway and bathroom, then sat on the edge of her bed and thought of all the things that had happened in one weekend. A dog laundry. A hide-out. Clogged pipes. A plumber's bill. A government crisis that was not a crisis. And a new problem: her mother had a boyfriend.

Angel sighed loudly. She was too tired to cry.

"Anyway," she said aloud to herself, "I had enough money to pay the plumber's bill, since it was our fault. And even money left over, forty-eight dollars."

She'd better not count her chickens, she thought. Or spend the money on something frivolous. Before long, she was sure, some crisis would come along where it would be needed.

SIX

Getting Ready for Rudy

While Angel was eating a late breakfast, Edna came to the door. "My mom is coming home today!" she said, bursting into the kitchen happily. She seemed to have forgotten about Angel's crisis.

"I know," said Angel, pouring more corn flakes into her bowl.

Edna chattered on as Angel ate. When she stopped, Angel told her they wouldn't need the hide-out and that their mother wasn't in any trouble after all.

"Not with the government, anyway," finished Angel, "but it's really worse: she has a boyfriend."

Edna frowned, thinking. She, like Angel, needed some time to adjust to a different crisis. "A boyfriend?" she said.

"Well, I suppose he is a man," said Angel. "And he is coming *here!*"

Edna whistled her long, low whistle. "It might be fun... Ginny Corbett's mother has a boyfriend."

Angel thought about Ginny Corbett. Her mother had always had a boyfriend. Ginny was used to him.

"Everything is going to change," said Angel gloomily. "How would you like it if *your* mother had a boyfriend? And started thinking about him and doing everything with him and she didn't even remember to cook dinner or take care of you..."

"My mother *does* have a boyfriend," said Edna cheerfully. "My dad!"

"Ha-ha," said Angel in mock humor. "Very funny."'

"Well, he is. She does stuff with him. Like now, she's out of town with him and didn't take me."

Somehow that didn't feel the same to Angel. And, anyway, Edna was too happy to understand. Her mother was coming home to hug her and care for her and make a fuss over her.

"And now that you have lots of money, you can run away from home!" said Edna cheerfully.

Angel told her about the plumber and the dog hair in the pipes.

"Well, you wouldn't really run away, anyway."

That was true. It didn't feel like the answer to Angel. Although she wouldn't mind having her mother miss her for a while. Then, when she returned, her mother would forget all about her boyfriend, she would be so glad to see Angel. She might even promise never to neglect her again. Angel could feel the warmth of the reunion...

Edna tried to be sympathetic and think of people at school whose mothers had boyfriends, but she soon lost interest and her attention wandered. "When is he coming?" she asked.

Angel sighed. "I don't know. Soon, I think."

Edna said she had to go home and watch for her mother, and she ran off, singing.

Mrs. O'Leary came back downstairs and poured Angel a glass of orange juice.

"Angel, I know you and Rags are going to love Rudy," she said. "He's so anxious to meet you."

Angel wondered why he would be anxious to meet them. What could he have in common with two small children?

"He's so funny, Angel. He has a wild sense of humor!" she went on.

Angel thought about the steering wheel story. If that's what her mother thought was funny, Angel decided she would do a lot of reading in her room while he was here.

"Where's he going to stay?" asked Rags. "Where will he sleep?"

"Why, I thought perhaps we would give him Angel's room. It's bright and sunny, and it's easier for children to sleep on the couch in the living room than for an adult."

It looked as though Angel wouldn't read in her room after all. Her room was going to be turned into a hotel for a perfect stranger. Her own sweet, private room, with all of her personal, private things in it. Her books, her diary, her stuffed animals, her toiletries.

"Rudy, Rudy, is a cootie!" sang Rags, who was in his making-up-a-rhyme mood again. "Rudy is moody, Rudy's a cootie," he went on.

"That's enough, Rags," said their mother.

Rags looked hurt. He thought his mother liked his rhymes. She usually liked everything he made up.

Not when they made fun of her new friend, thought Angel. Her mother must like this man a lot if she disapproved of Rags' making up rhymes about him. She usually let him make up rhymes about anyone. Now Angel *was* worried.

He was even more important to her mother than Angel had feared.

"It will be fun to have a houseguest, won't it?" said their mother brightly.

When the children did not respond, she said, "We hardly ever have company — it will be good for us. You just wait — you'll see how much fun he is."

Why was it so important to her mother that they like him? Angel could feel her mother pushing them together with this strange man. After all, he was just a visitor — and their mother's visitor at that. Why couldn't they feel free to keep their distance? But their mother had a pleading look in her eyes.

"When is he coming?" asked Angel politely.

"Next week, Angel. Next Sunday. And we have so much to do beforehand. Why, we have to clean and wax the floor and get food in the house and the curtains should be laundered and the yard cleaned up..."

Angel couldn't remember when their mother

had been that concerned over the housework and the yard. And the curtains had been laundered just before Alyce had come to stay. They couldn't be dirty already.

"I'll help!" said Rags, anxious to reinstate himself in his mother's graces. "I'll clean up the yard!"

"Good!" said their mother. "And Angel can help me around the house. Oh dear, I don't know where to begin!" Their mother looked in a dither.

"Doesn't Rudy work?" asked Angel.

"I told you, dear, he's between jobs. He has a chance to travel now, before he begins something new."

That could mean he had all the time in the world, thought Angel. He may never leave! Angel grew nervous. She liked to think someone was waiting for his return. That he had, say, a two-week vacation.

"What is he?" demanded Rags. "Is he a teacher or a milkman or a policeman or a fireman?"

Rags had a new book about the neighborhood helpers. It had large, colorful pictures of all kinds of workers.

"Or a preacher?" he added. "A teacher or a preacher! Preacher-teacher, teacher-preacher!" Rags hoped to redeem himself with his new rhyme.

As Mrs. O'Leary cleared the breakfast dishes from the table, she said, "He's a clown."

The children both looked up at her. Their mouths fell open and they didn't say anything. Whatever Angel had thought he might be, this wasn't it. Perhaps her mother meant he was a "clown," just a funny fellow.

"You mean he's really funny," said Angel. "But what does he do for a living?"

"He's a clown," repeated Mrs. O'Leary. "He's in the entertainment field."

Having a mother with a boyfriend was one thing. But having a mother with a boyfriend who happened to be a clown was humiliating. No one had a boyfriend who was a clown. Not

Ginny Corbett's mother, not anybody. People didn't have clowns for friends. They had lawyers and teachers and clerks and sometimes students or secretaries, but not clowns.

Now here was their own mother, with her hands in the soapy dishwater, talking about Rudy the clown as if it was a perfectly normal thing to be.

"...and then he got this job in Washington, D.C. It started with work at parties, you know — Washington has a lot of parties — and then he went to work on television, he had a show with another clown named Rita — you know, a show for children, Rags — and he did a very good job, but he did it for four years and then he felt he'd done all he could — I mean, there were no surprises left — and he wanted some change in his life, so he quit. He'd saved some money, and he took a trip to Canada to see how he'd like it there, and that's where your Aunt Beth and I met him!"

Mrs. O'Leary stopped for breath and to push

her hair back from her forehead with a soapy hand.

Why didn't he go see Aunt Beth? Angel wondered. And it seemed quite irresponsible to just quit a job and go traveling all over Canada, willy-nilly, no job at all to go back to.

As if reading Angel's thoughts, their mother went on, "He really needs to find a job now, but since he is out of work anyway, he thought this would be a good time to come and see us... before he settles down somewhere else..."

"Is he going to see Aunt Beth, too?" asked Angel.

Mrs. O'Leary blushed. Angel could see her face turning pink, but she thought maybe it was just from the steam at the sink.

"I don't think so, Angel. I mean, he liked us *both*, of course, but he seemed to...ah..."

"Like you best?" finished Rags.

"Well, don't get me wrong, he likes your Aunt Beth, too, Rags, but he took a sort of fancy to me. They used to say that."

Angel knew very well what that meant. Rudy the clown was more than a friend. He liked her mother like a girlfriend and she liked him like a boyfriend. They were what Angel had read in her *How Your Body Changes* book, "physically attracted to each other."

Angel felt weak all over. Her mother was in love with a clown! Rags was taking all of this far too well, laughing and stumbling around like a clown. Now he had his crayons out at the table and was drawing circles on his nose!

"Look at me!" he cried, outlining his lips with red crayon.

Angel was too dumbfounded to say a word. If only she was faced with kidnappers again it would seem trivial. *This* was a problem that could last a lifetime!

Her mother finished the dishes and wiped off the table, then came over and put her arms around Angel and Rags.

"It will all work out just fine," she said. "Rudy will come and visit and he will leave and go back to Washington and our life will probably go on just as usual. You don't have anything to worry about, Angel."

Those were the most sensible words her mother had said in weeks. The possibility that he would come (and they would hate him) and go back to Washington (and be forgotten)... Angel dared to breathe a sigh of relief.

All week long the children helped their mother clean and prepare dinners for the freezer and touch up the paint where it was peeling on the woodwork. Mrs. O'Leary bought new tiebacks for the kitchen curtains and shook the rugs in Angel's room and hung a new picture on the wall. Alyce came and helped her move furniture and dust in places that had never been dusted before. Edna came and helped Angel clear out her bureau drawers so Rudy would have a place to put his clothes — pantaloons? shoes three sizes too large?

It all seemed like a lot of work to Angel, when he was staying for such a short time. And for almost a complete stranger, even if he was physically attracted to their mother.

Their mother seemed to look younger every day. By the end of the week she had tied her hair back in ponytails and her face was rosy and almost freckled. She could have been Angel's

sister. Angel had to admit that it was nice to see her mother so happy. Perhaps the whole family had to suffer some for happiness.

By Sunday, everything was in tiptop shape, and fresh flowers stood in a vase on Angel's night table. The only thing left to do was to sit

on the couch in good clothes and listen for a car to drive up and stop at the curb, where Alyce usually parked her car.

And driving that car all the way from Washington, D.C., would be Rudy the clown, their mother's boyfriend.

SEVEN

A Clown Comes to Stay

"There he is!" said Mrs. O'Leary. "There's Rudy, Angel and Rags!"

She and Rags tumbled over each other to get to the door, but Angel sat on the couch quietly. She was afraid to look out the window for fear that the car was one of those that came apart in the middle, or a small foreign car that would dispense person after person until a hundred men were standing beside it. Surely a clown did not drive a normal family car.

"Angel!" called her mother from the side yard, "come out and meet Rudy!"

Angel knew she could not put it off any longer. As she started for the door, she had a sudden hopeful thought. Clowns were not clowns all the time. They went to work, like doctors or teachers. They only did funny things at work. Then they changed their clothes and came home like regular people. In fact, Angel remembered, she had read something about how most clowns were very sad, quiet people and the reason they became clowns was so they could act happy even though they were not.

Angel felt better, remembering this, and when she got to the door, she knew she was right. There, standing on their front sidewalk, was a tall young man reaching down to shake Rags's hand solemnly. He did not have baggy pants on! His shoes were not floppy! He was wearing jeans and had plain brown loafers on normal-sized feet! The car in the background had no flowers or decorations on it, it was not split in two, and there were no small men crawling out of its doors.

Angel ran down the porch steps with relief, but just as she got to the bottom, the hand Rags was shaking came off in his own and he squealed in alarm. A fake hand. The oldest joke in the world. Rags was putting the hand over his own now and reaching out to Angel to shake hands with her.

"Angel, dear, this is Rudy," said their mother, flushed and rosy from all the excitement. "Rudy, this is my daughter, Angel."

Angel kept her hands behind her back. "Hello," she said.

Rudy made a sweeping bow in front of Angel and whipped a giant bouquet of fresh flowers out of his shirtsleeve and handed them to her. "For you," he said. "And I'm pleased to meet you, Angel."

What did a person say to a clown? Did you thank him for magic flowers? Or did you return them so that he could use them again for another trick?

"Let's put those flowers in water," said her

mother, answering her unspoken questions.

They all trooped into the house, and Rags carried Rudy's bags up to Angel's room. Then they sat down at the dining room table and Mrs. O'Leary made some tea and set out some sandwiches and cookies.

Mrs. O'Leary chattered away, asking questions about the trip, and while she was talking, Rudy made the plate of cookies disappear. Rags was beside himself with excitement. He looked under the table and under the tablecloth and, finally, all over the dining room. From there he went to the kitchen and on to the living room in his search. When he came back to the table, the cookies were right where they had been before!

"Where were they?" shouted Rags. "Where were the cookies?"

Rudy looked surprised. "They were right here," he said. "Right here on the table."

Angel and her mother laughed politely, and Rags looked as if a trick had been played on him. He didn't like to be laughed at.

"They were right here on my knees," said Rudy kindly. "Under the tablecloth."

He must have done that very fast, thought Angel. She didn't see him take the plate or put it back. Clowns must be like magicians, only they dress funnier.

While Rudy talked about driving on the Pennsylvania Turnpike and Angel and her mother listened attentively, Rags slipped from his chair and walked around to his mother. He tugged on her sleeve and said in a loud whisper, "I thought you said he was a *clown*..."

Mrs. O'Leary did not appear to hear him, so he said in a louder voice, "You said he was a clown...He doesn't look like a clown. He hasn't got a hat and white paint on and big shoes."

"Rudy is a clown at *work*, Rags," his mother said, "just like a fireman or a policeman. They wear their uniforms at work, and when they come home, they put on regular clothes."

Rags stared at Rudy. Rudy smiled and nodded.

Then he went on talking about the Pennsylvania Turnpike.

Rags went back to his chair and sulked. He had been promised a genuine clown, and this man looked perfectly ordinary, even when he made cookies disappear.

There was a knock on the back door, and Angel let Edna in. "My mom wants to know if she can borrow some vanilla," she said clearly, looking at Rudy all the while.

"Why, of course, dear," said Mrs. O'Leary. "Angel, you know where the vanilla is. You get it for her."

"This is Rudy," said Rags, pointing.

Rudy stood up and shook Edna's hand. Then he sat down and talked about the turnpike again, and Angel and Edna went into the kitchen.

"I thought you said he was a *clown!*" said Edna. "He doesn't look like a clown to me."

"He's not a full-time clown," said Angel, looking for the vanilla. "He doesn't wear his clown suit unless he's working."

Angel was extremely relieved that he didn't wear baggy pants and floppy shoes in public... or in private. Disappearing cookies and magic flowers were one thing: *looking* like a clown was quite another.

But Edna looked as let down as Rags. "He could at least have one of those flowers in his button-hole that squirts water when you smell it."

Edna took the vanilla and left, looking disappointed. Right after Angel had sat down at the table to hear more about Rudy's trip (which she found just a bit boring), the back door opened after a *tap-tap* on it sounded, and Alyce stuck her head partway in.

"What has four wheels and flies?" she said with a bright smile on her face.

All four people at the table looked at her in surprise. What in the world was she doing? thought Angel. And why didn't she say hello first?

As they all stared at her, she repeated the question. When no one responded, she said,

"Give up?" She looked from one to the other brightly. "A garbage truck!" she said. "Four wheels and flies! Get it?"

Now Alyce came all the way in and closed the door.

"You must be Rudy," she said, reaching across the table to shake his hand.

Rudy stood up and shook her hand and said, "I'm pleased to meet you," as Angel's mother said, "This is Alyce."'

"I get it, Alyce!" shouted Rags. "Four wheels and flies! A garbage truck!"

"Just a little clowning when I'm introduced to a clown!" replied Alyce.

Angel thought with relief that it was good she hadn't come in with a party hat on her head or throwing a pail of confetti that she pretended was water. She wondered if anyone else would come by to meet Rudy. She couldn't think of anyone else who knew he was coming.

Alyce sat down and had a cup of tea and listened to the rest of Rudy's travelogue. She laughed uproariously when he told of a flat tire in Ohio and a thunderstorm in Michigan. Rags began to laugh, too, but Angel and her mother didn't see anything very funny about the stories.

After a while Mrs. O'Leary cleared the table and said, "Perhaps Rudy would like to rest after the long drive."

Rudy admitted he would, and Mrs. O'Leary showed him Angel's room, and Alyce said good-bye and went home.

Angel helped her mother do the dishes while Rags sat under the table trying to make the salt and pepper shakers disappear.

"Do you like him, Angel?" said her mother. "Isn't he funny and nice?"

Angel nodded cautiously. She didn't want to make any commitment about Rudy yet.

"He's nice," she said. "But I don't know if I like him yet. I don't really know him very well."

Her mother laughed and ruffled Angel's hair. "That's my Angel," she said. "So serious about everything."

Angel wondered how her mother could take something like this so lightly. It was their very lives she was talking about. Rudy could change the very way they lived. And that was surely no joke. It was very, very serious. Her mother was so lighthearted about everything lately, she was practically frivolous.

Rudy was funny, she admitted, thinking about the fake hand and the flowers, even if they were the oldest jokes in the world. And at least he wasn't going to be an embarrassment by wearing funny clothes around the house. But beyond that, Angel would make no judgment — yet.

EIGHT

Pea Green Shoes

After a few days Rudy settled in. Having a live-in clown was not too disturbing to Angel. He acted like any other visitor and took the family out for dinner and to the zoo and played lots of games with Rags.

On Halloween, he dressed up like a tea bag, with a little string coming out of his head with the label on it, and he dressed Angel like a green bean by sewing the legs of some old green pajamas together and cutting off the arms altogether. It was a tight, warm costume but it drew many comments, and everyone remarked how much like a real green bean she looked.

Rags was dressed like an Oreo cookie, and when they went from door to door for tricks or treats, everyone said he looked sweet enough to eat. After trick or treating, Rudy took them to the party at City Hall, where Angel won second prize for her costume. She had to admit it was one of the best Halloweens she'd ever had, and even the costume Edna's mother had bought her wasn't nearly as effective or original.

Rudy also took Mrs. O'Leary dancing and to plays in the city, so Alyce came to baby-sit many evenings. Angel had to admit it was a good thing to see their mother happy, although between going to work and going out with Rudy, she was not home as much as she used to be with the children. Mrs. O'Leary called the time they did spend together "quality time."

"Before Rudy came I was always home, but we didn't *enjoy* each other as much, Angel.

Now we have *quality* time together, instead of quantity time."

What she meant, thought Angel, was that because she was so happy going out with Rudy, some of this happiness was rubbing off on the children. She *was* more fun to be with. Angel sighed. Being a child with a mother was so complicated.

Angel was surprised to find that the thing that bothered her the most about Rudy's being there was that she missed having her own room. Not that she hadn't expected to miss it, but it surprised her that her room would be the only real problem. On the way home from school one afternoon, she told Edna about it.

"All my things are in boxes, and I can't read in bed, and I don't like to wear my pajamas in the living room."

Edna gave her full attention to Angel's problem, since she had none of her own at the moment. Her parents were safely back in the house and her hair and clothes were back to normal.

"How long do you think he'll stay?" said Edna.

"I don't know," said Angel. "He looks like he is sort of settled. Like he lives here."

"Maybe he should rent a room in town," said Edna. "Or maybe your mom should add on a room or something..."

"He isn't going to be here *that* long!" said Angel in alarm.

"Then maybe he should have Rags's room," said Edna.

"Rags has a junior bed," said Angel. "Rudy wouldn't fit in it. And all Rags's toys are all over. It wouldn't work."

The girls reached Angel's back porch and sat down on the steps.

"I think the best thing," said Edna thoughtfully, "is to ask your mom how long he intends to stay. Then you can plan when you'll have your room back again. I mean, it's something to look forward to, and you can mark it on your calendar."

"My calendar is in my room," said Angel gloomily. She had hoped that Edna would have a good, clear-cut solution, the way she did to so many other problems.

"Maybe you could move to the basement, or the attic, or the hide-out," Edna said, to show she was still thinking. "Come and stay with me."

Angel shook her head. She didn't want her mother to feel guilty or to stop having a good time or to think she minded having a house-guest. "That would look as though I wasn't satisfied," she said.

"You aren't," said Edna.

"I don't want to *upset* things," said Angel. "I think you're right. The best idea is to find out how long he's staying and then count the days till I get my room back. It'll be like a goal."

Both girls were familiar with goals in school. Their teachers were always talking about setting goals.

"Are those new sneakers?" said Angel, changing the subject.

Edna nodded. "My mom brought them back from the trip. These bright colors are really popular this spring. They're in all the stores."

Angel looked at Edna's shoes and wished she had some like them. They looked like yellow Easter eggs.

"Pastels," Edna went on. "They come in yellow, like these, and violet and light blue and aqua and pink and lime. Just like jelly beans."

Angel looked down at her own scuffed white ones. They had looked all right that morning, but now they looked old and dirty compared to Edna's new ones.

"Why don't you dye yours?" said Edna. "They would be just like new again. It's easy to dye sneakers."

"Really?" said Angel. She grew interested. It would be something to do to take her mind off her room.

"Let's go to the store and get some dye!" said Edna, jumping up from the steps.

"Maybe I should ask my mom," said Angel.

"She's not home, is she?"

The house had been very quiet. Angel tried the back door. It was locked.

"I guess not," said Angel. "There's probably a note inside."

"Then let's go to the store!" said Edna impatiently. "You can surprise your mom. Show her when she gets home."

Angel looked down at Edna's jelly bean shoes. Then she looked at her own common, scuffed white ones.

"All right," she said. "I'll have to go in and get some money."

Angel unlocked the door and got a dollar bill from her room and read the note her mother had left.

"Rudy and Rags and I are shopping downtown. Will be home soon. Love, Mother."

There should be time to get the dye and dye my shoes before they got home, Angel thought.

When Edna and Angel got to the drugstore,

they looked at the little packets of colorful dyes lined up in the rack. There were so many colors, it was hard for Angel to choose.

"I'd choose Paragon Pink," said Edna. "Or maybe this one. Rambling Rose."

"I don't like pink," said Angel. "It reminds me of babies."

Edna shrugged her shoulders. "How about Cerulean Blue?"

Angel wrinkled her nose. She liked blue. But she had something brighter in mind, like Edna's shoes.

"Here!" she said, picking up exactly the color she wanted.

"Chartreuse?" said Edna. "Do you like chartreuse?"

Angel nodded. "It looks just like a Popsicle," she said. "A lime Popsicle."

Angel paid for the dye, and the girls ran to Angel's house and read the directions on the envelope.

"Add four quarts of boiling water to contents

in envelope," read Edna. "We'll need a big pan."

Angel ran to the pantry and got her mother's biggest cooking pan. She measured four quarts of water with a mason jar and set the pan on the stove to boil. The pan covered two gas burners.

Before long it came to a roaring boil, and Angel turned off the burners and emptied the envelope of powdered dye into the water. As if by magic, the water turned to a bright lime green lake.

"Wow!" said Edna. "It looks just like lime Jell-O!"

"It looks good enough to eat," said Angel. "I mean drink. Maybe it tastes like lime Kool-Aid."

Angel stirred the lime lake with a large metal spoon, as the envelope suggested. The dye dissolved quickly, and Edna read, "Immerse the article in the liquid, being sure to move it about to prevent spotting."' Angel put the shoes in.

Then she read on: "Wear rubber gloves to prevent the skin from being stained by dye.

This dye conforms to the Pure Food and Drug Act and is not dangerous when swallowed."

Angel pulled on her mother's dishwashing gloves and moved the shoes around cautiously in the liquid.

"Let's let them sit in it for a while," said Edna, "to be sure they get dark enough."

"Look at all the dye we have left over," said Angel. "We could dye all kinds of things besides my shoes..."

She and Edna glanced around the kitchen. There were curtains and dish towels and aprons and of course the girls' own blouses.

Angel felt dubious. "Lime is nice for sneakers," she said, "but it wouldn't match the kitchen walls."

"We may need all of the dye to get the sneakers just the right color," added Edna.

Angel lifted one shoe out of the pan, gently, with the metal spoon. It wasn't lime. It looked gray and wet.

"I think it needs a long time," said Edna.

"Let's do our homework while we're waiting."

The girls went into the dining room and did their geography together. Then they wrote an essay on foods that have protein in them, for health class. When they finished that, they played a game of Monopoly. While they were watching a rerun of *The Brady Bunch* on TV, Edna's mother called to say it was almost suppertime.

"The shoes!" cried Angel. She ran to the kitchen and lifted one from the pan. Far from lime green, the shoe dripped from the spoon, gray and dank.

"It's not chartreuse!" said Edna. "That package was mismarked!"

Angel looked despondent. "The water looks lime," she said.

Edna looked at the package. "Launder article before dyeing," she read. "It's in small print. Do you think that's what's the matter?"

"The shoes weren't *that* dirty," said Angel. "But they aren't lime. They're kind of mud green."

"Pea green," said Edna. "Like pea soup."

"They aren't pastel," said Angel sadly. "They don't look like a jelly bean or a Popsicle or an Easter egg."

"Maybe it's because they're wet!" said Edna

suddenly. "Maybe when they dry, they *will* be lime green!"

Angel wanted to believe that, and she tried to. She said "Maybe" to Edna, but she didn't feel a bit hopeful.

After Edna left, Angel put the shoes into the dryer and turned it to High. As she cleaned up the kitchen, she noticed that although the dye did not make the shoes lime green, it had colored everything else it had touched. There were splashes of lime on the cupboard and wall and table and chair, and Angel scrubbed them off with cleanser. When the dryer stopped, she took out her hot, dry shoes. Being dry did not make them lime green. They were still pea green, only muddier.

Angel put them on and sat down to watch TV until her mother and Rudy and Rags came home.

Ten minutes later they burst in the door, Rags waving a clown puppet with flaming red hair. Her mother looked flushed and happy and said,

"Get your jacket on, Angel. We're going out to Smiley's for dinner!"

Angel liked Smiley's. It was a new fast-food restaurant in town.

On the way out to dinner, her mother said, "Why, Angel, what happened to your shoes? Did you walk through something on the way home from school?"

Angel blushed. "We dyed them. Edna and me."

Her mother frowned. Rags shouted, "They look like spinach." He made a face.

Rudy said, "They look fine to me!"

"Those shoes were still good, Angel. They had a lot of wear in them yet." Her mother sounded like her old self again, like a regular mother. And she meant that Angel wasn't going to get new shoes just because she experimented on these.

At Smiley's Rudy said that Angel and Rags could have anything to eat on the menu. "My treat," he said. "Look," he added, shaking his arm and sending forth a clatter of coins on the table. Rags shrieked. He tried to do the same thing, but shake as hard as he could, no money came from Rags's shirt.

As Angel ate her Big Smiley and thick chocolate milk shake, she noticed that they looked like a family. A regular mother and father and two children, a boy and a girl. She always used to think she wanted that when she was small. But having their mother to themselves got to be a very nice, warm thing, and she began to feel sorry for children who had to share.

So far, though, sharing hadn't been so bad. They got to do more things, and their mother was happier.

If only she could have her own room back.

NINE

A Job and a Room for Rudy

Angel wore her pea green shoes to school, and after the first few comments, no one paid any attention to them. Angel kept envying Edna's yellow ones and tried to wear the toes of hers out. When they had holes in them, she thought she would ask her mother if she could use a little of the dog wash money to buy new ones.

On the way to school one morning, Edna said, "Did you ask your mother yet? Did you ask her how long Rudy was staying?"

"I'll ask her tonight," said Angel. Actually,

Angel had mixed feelings about Rudy's staying. He was beginning to fit in, and he did work around the house, whistling and singing. He was building Rags a garage for his Matchbox cars and making Angel a dressing table with a chintz skirt around it. He fixed things that were broken and put a fence around Mrs. O'Leary's small garden. He didn't act like a clown too often, and he didn't try to take their mother away from them.

But Angel did wonder about her room, and just when she had worked up enough courage to ask her mother when she would have it back, she found out.

One evening her mother burst in the door and said to the children, "Guess what? Rudy has a *job!* The television station offered him a small show for children. Isn't that wonderful?"

Angel felt different emotions jostling for attention, as usual. A job was good. He would earn money. But would he live in her room forever? Maybe Edna was right — they should add a room onto the house for Rudy. And what about his job? It was one thing to be a clown in private, an unemployed clown. It would be quite another thing to be a clown on television, where the children who watched him were Angel's own classmates!

Rudy was swinging Rags over his head.

"It's just an afternoon show, three days a week," their mother said. "Only an hour long. But the pay is good, and the experience will be wonderful. You can see Rudy on TV, Rags!"

"Then Rudy isn't going home at all?" said Angel. "He's going to stay here forever?"

Rudy turned to Angel. "I have no job to go back to," he said seriously. "And I like it here very much. So when I heard about this job, and the producer liked my act, it seemed like a good idea to stay for a while. I'll rent a room downtown, so that I won't disturb the family. You need a room of your own."

Angel heard herself asking, "Will you come and see us?"

"Yes," he said, "I'd like to see you."

"That's why he took the job, Angel!" Mrs. O'Leary said. "So he could come and see us. He could be nearby, but have a place of his own."

Angel was relieved. This job seemed to solve both the problem of Rudy's leaving and his staying. He wouldn't have to leave, but Angel could have her room back. The only thing left to worry about (and there was always something) was having everyone see her mother's boyfriend in a clown suit. Who knew what he might do on an hour-long show?

That evening Rudy looked through the Rooms for Rent in the paper and circled all the possibilities in red pencil. The next afternoon, while their mother was at work, Angel and Rags went with Rudy to find a room.

"No children," said the woman at the first house they visited.

"We aren't going to live here," said Angel quickly.

"No, thank you," said Rudy politely. Then

he added to Angel as they walked away, "I wouldn't want to stay at a place where they don't like children, even if you won't be living there. I want you to be able to come and visit as often as you like."

Rags slipped his hand into Rudy's and muttered, "Mean lady."

It scared Angel a little bit to notice how close to Rudy Rags had become. Since Rudy hadn't been working, he took Rags with him every day when he went out. Angel had noticed how much more free time she had and how both she and her mother were sharing the responsibility of Rags's life with Rudy. On the one hand, it was wonderful. On the other, thought Angel, what would happen when Rudy left? He was surely bound to leave someday. Even their own father had left, and this man was a complete stranger. Angel didn't like to think about it, but she knew it was true. He could leave at any time.

What would Rags do then? What would her

mother do then? Angel realized that she was the only one who wasn't dependent on Rudy.

They looked at several rooms together, and in between they had an ice cream cone at Curly-Maid.

As they licked their ice cream, Rudy said, "I think the next room I look at will be the one — the perfect room."

And sure enough it was! Angel wondered if all clowns knew magic. Rudy seemed to have magical powers, the way it said in the ESP books she had read in the library.

The room was near the television station. It was fully furnished, had a small kitchen, and faced south.

"I like a room that faces south," said Rudy. "Sun all year long. Good for my plants." He wrote out a check and handed it to the landlord. "I'll move in on Saturday," he told him.

On the way home, Rudy showed them the studio where he would be working. It was just a small room with chairs, for this was a small television station, the only one in town.

All week Rudy got ready for his first show, and Angel and Rags helped him. Angel told him what she thought was funny. Rags said someone should throw a pie in his face, and Angel said no.

Rags and Angel and Edna also helped Rudy paint a set for the background. The television station didn't have anything suitable.

On the afternoon of the first show, Angel's mother took time off from work to sit in the front row with Angel and Rags and Alyce and Edna. Even Margaret Toomer came. In back of them were chairs full of children from Angel's school. Excitement mounted as the red lights flashed and the cameras drew in to focus on Rudy's entrance. The applause sounded very, very loud to Angel, probably because the room was small. As the children clapped and hooted, Rudy came running out onto the stage.

Even though Angel had helped write the jokes and get ready for the show, there were lots of surprises. They had never seen Rudy dressed up before. This was not the Rudy Angel knew — this could have been anyone. It was a stranger up on the stage, and even Rags felt shy and bashful. The stranger had something tight over his head that was painted red, white, and blue, with tufts of red yarn hair sticking out of it. On his face was a giant, bulbous red nose, and circles were painted on his cheeks like bull's-eyes. His ears were large and floppy, and around his neck was a huge, spotted necktie that hung clear down to his giant floppy shoes. Rope suspenders held the loose pants up. A bouquet of flowers was tucked into the band of his straw hat. He told jokes and read the children stories and did magic tricks, and near the end he did a dance while a small band of clowns accompanied him on old kettles and drums.

In the middle of the dance, the drummer played a rousing fanfare, and Rudy leaned over the edge of the stage and motioned for Angel and Rags to come up.

Rags flew out of his seat and into Rudy's arms, but Angel pretended not to see him and looked the other way. She was worried enough about what her classmates would say at school the next day — she didn't want to be a clown, too.

But when she turned to look back, she saw that Rudy was coming down the steps and into the audience! He bowed low in front of her (oh, how embarrassing! The spotlight and camera were on her!) and said, "May I have this dance, young lady?" and swept Angel to her feet and onto the stage!

As the other clowns played their music, Rudy danced around the stage with Angel. When they were finished, the applause was thunderous, and Rudy said some words of thanks to Angel and Rags and Edna for helping him all week long. Angel turned bright red (was it the hot lights?), Rags acted like a clown, and Edna stood up and bowed.

Then the whole audience, including Angel and Rags and their mother and Alyce and Edna and

Margaret Toomer, dashed home quickly to see themselves on television! The show had been recorded on tape, to be broadcast an hour later.

Angel felt intense excitement at being on TV.

"Just like the Brady Bunch!" shouted Rags, as the show started.

Angel also felt intense embarrassment now, and she was afraid to look at the screen and see herself.

There they were! The camera panned the audience and showed Edna waving at the camera, Alyce smiling, Margaret Toomer looking serious.

And Rudy, a real clown, on the stage in front of them!

"Here I am! Here I am!" screamed Rags.

Angel watched with her hands over one eye as she, Angel O'Leary, was swept up onto the stage and danced with Rudy the clown, their mother's boyfriend!

"Those shoes!" shouted her mother. "You should have worn your dress shoes, Angel!"

Her mother was right. There were those awful

pea green shoes with the spotlight on them, highlighting their pea-greeniness!

At school the next day, Angel waited for jokes and teasing. Instead of that, she realized that she and Edna were celebrities!

"I wish my dad was a clown," said one of the girls in her class.

"We're going to get tickets and go to the studio every week," said a boy.

"Perhaps Angel could write a report on what it's like to have a clown for a friend," said her teacher. "She could give it when we talk about careers next week."

Angel felt her face turning red, and there were no lights at school. Not hot ones. She never thought of being a clown as something one made a career of. Still, if the teacher said so . . .

On Saturday Rudy moved into his new room and Angel moved back upstairs. That evening she looked at her familiar things, all neatly in place, and was glad she had shared her room. It felt so much better to come back to it when she'd been away. And there were surprises everywhere. When she was putting her socks into the drawer, she found a candy bar. When she opened her jewelry box, she found a new bracelet. Pinned onto her curtain, when she pulled down her shade that evening, was a set of clothes for her Barbie doll.

"Magic!" she said out loud.

And when she thought of magic, she knew it was Rudy.

That night she slept soundly, and in the morning when she woke up, right beside her bed where she had left her pea green sneakers, were different sneakers. Lime green, chartreuse as could be, new, bright, pastel, jelly bean sneakers! And the pea green ones were gone!

Angel dressed in a hurry and tried the lime green shoes on. They just fit! She ran down to the kitchen, where her mother was getting oatmeal ready for breakfast.

"Thank you!" she said.

Her mother turned around. Angel pointed to the shoes.

"They aren't from me," said Mrs. O'Leary.

"From Rudy!" said Angel.

Angel thanked Rudy when he came over later that day. At last she could stop being embarrassed about her sneakers. These were shoes she could be proud of!

TEN

Christmas Without Rudy

Angel wore her new sneakers to school every day until the snow fell. On Thanksgiving, Rudy cooked a turkey in the small stove in his small kitchen and the family crowded around a card table laden with cranberries and sweet potatoes and pumpkin pie.

"It's my turn to cook!" Rudy said. "We'll just have to squeeze!"

They did squeeze, and it was just as much fun as if they had been in a large room. In fact, more, thought Angel. There was something about having Rudy there (she had to admit) that made everything into a party. The family found that out for sure at Christmas.

On the day after Thanksgiving, Rudy said, "In the last letter I got from my mother and dad, they sounded lonely. I miss them, too, and I think maybe I should spend Christmas with them in Greece."

Angel and Rags and their mother looked shocked. They knew, of course, that Rudy had a family of his own, but he didn't talk about them often. Angel didn't realize how accustomed she had become to thinking of Rudy's home as near them.

"I'd like to take you all along to meet them," he said.

Mrs. O'Leary shook her head. "We'd love to come if we could, but I can't take time from work," she said.

The three O'Learys looked wistful. "It won't be any fun without Rudy at Christmas," whined Rags.

"We always were alone before," said his

mother. "We'll have a nice Christmas with just the three of us."

"I'll miss you all a lot," said Rudy. "But my parents are getting old and I'd like to have a nice visit with them."

"I think it's a good idea," said Mrs. O'Leary. "It's only fair that you spend some time with your family. You go and have a good time and hurry back."

Rudy began to talk about his trip to Greece and to call airlines for reservations. He and Angel and Rags shopped for Christmas presents for his family, and he borrowed a big suitcase to carry all the packages in. "They'll be so glad to see me!" he said. "I can't wait to tell them all about you and show them pictures of the family."

Angel tried and tried to get into the spirit of Christmas. After they drove Rudy to the airport and said good-bye, they bought a Christmas tree and set it up in the living room. Mrs. O'Leary strung lights on it, and Rags and Angel trimmed it with ornaments and popcorn and cranberry strings. Even though there was Christmas music on the phonograph, Angel did not feel like Christmas.

"Aren't we lucky our family is all together!" said their mother brightly on Christmas Day. She put her arms around the children and hugged them. "Our own little family," she said.

"Rudy's not here," said Rags. "I want Rudy."

"Grow up, Rags," said Angel crossly. "Rudy has to be with his own family sometimes."

"He could have taken us along," said Rags with a sob.

"Mom couldn't get time from work," said Angel impatiently. "And we can't leave Mom alone on Christmas."

Even opening presents that were chosen so carefully lacked something this year. There was a sort of hole, an empty spot, inside.

"Last year we had a fine Christmas alone!" said their mother.

"We didn't know Rudy then," said Angel.

"It isn't good to be dependent on other people," said their mother sensibly. "Everyone has to have a life of his or her own." She looked sad as she said it.

"I want Rudy," wailed Rags.

"Let's go out for Christmas dinner," said their mother brightly. "We'll eat turkey in a restaurant, where people are."

The children felt a surge of excitement for a

moment and put on their warm coats. When they got to the restaurant, it was decorated festively with pine cones and trees and garlands of tinsel. But not many people were there.

"They're at home with their families and friends," said Angel.

"We have our family right here!"' said their mother, looking at the menu. "And our friends are with their own families."

It was true. Alyce had gone to her niece's house. Margaret Toomer was at her daughter's in Milwaukee. Rudy was in Greece. Edna was at her grandmother's on a farm in the country with all of her cousins.

Their mother ordered turkey for all of them.

"Isn't this good?" she said. Rags chewed listlessly on a drumstick.

Angel said, "Yes," but thought it was not nearly as good as Rudy's turkey had been on Thanksgiving, all sizzling and hot from his oven. This tasted dry and restauranty, and the cranberries tasted as though they had come out of a can instead of off the stove. And Rudy's gravy had been thick and creamy.

Or maybe it wasn't the food at all, thought Angel. Maybe it was Rudy with his apron on, singing and teasing. Maybe it was his sparkling eyes and his kindness. Maybe it was having Rudy there that made any food taste good.

That night in bed in her new pajamas, Angel began to worry about Rudy in Greece. Would he find he liked to be home again and decide to stay? Would he say to his mother, in Greek, "Boy, I didn't realize how much I missed things around here!" Would his dad put his arm on his shoulder and say, "I'm not too well, Son. Maybe you should come here, where you are closer to us."

Or, worse yet, perhaps Rudy would go to Washington on the way home. Or maybe he'd meet an old school friend...She could hear him in her mind...

"Why, Carol! Are you back in town?"

"Yes, I just quit my job in Utah and came

home. But it's lonely here...My friends are gone..."

"Well, I'll be in town over the holidays, let's get together!"

Now Angel saw Carol dancing with Rudy, clinging to him as dancers do...They would stop under some mistletoe and Carol would lean up and smile...What else could Rudy do? He would have to kiss her.

Maybe Carol's father owned a bank in town and needed a banker. "You could do the job, Son," he would say to Rudy. "I'll give you a good job with lots of benefits..."

Washington was exciting, more exciting than Wisconsin. He would take it! Angel knew he would take the job Carol's father offered him!

Angel heard the phone ring. It was Rudy! Telling her mother that he wasn't coming back. Telling her to close up his room and send him his clothes and plants. Angel ran down the stairs two at; a time.

"Hello!" their mother was saying, and she

winked. "Yes, yes, she's right here," she said, handing Angel the phone.

It *was* Rudy!

"Did you take it? Did you take the job in the bank?"

Rudy began to laugh. Angel's mother could hear him laughing across the room. "What job, Angel?"

"The job Carol's dad offered you."

"I've got a job in Wisconsin, Angel. And I don't know anyone named Carol. I wanted to say Merry Christmas and that I love you."

Angel's mother took the phone then and said that Rags was sound asleep. Then they talked while Angel went back to her room and scolded herself for having such a wild imagination. Rudy was in Greece, visiting his parents. Couldn't she learn to control her worries? She knew she was wrong most of the time!

Another thing that surprised Angel now was that she realized how much she cared for Rudy. He had brought such joy into the house, he had given them spirit and enthusiasm, he had brought fun into their lives! But her mother was right — they were beginning to *depend* on him! Surely Rags and her mother were. Why! What a fuss Rags made at dinner! And she could see that her mother was listless, too, even though she pretended to be happy.

Just the same, knowing Rudy would be back, and remembering his words "I love you" warmed Angel on Christmas night, and she fell asleep happier than she had been since Rudy had left.

On New Year's Day, Rudy returned, and blew into the house bringing back all the cheer that had been missing. He brought suitcases filled with gifts and Greek cakes and candies for all of them. He threw Rags up onto his shoulder, and Rags squealed and laughed and pretended to pull Rudy's hair. They went for a long walk in the snow, and then they went sliding, all four of them, on the big hill behind the high school.

"I really missed you," said Rudy as they all walked home to make hot cocoa.

The next morning at breakfast, as her mother poured orange juice for her, Angel said, "Remember that question you asked me that day Rudy first came?"

Her mother looked puzzled.

"The one that I said it was too soon to answer then," added Angel. "Well, I can answer it now. The answer is that I do."

ELEVEN

Rudy Saves the Day

After the holiday festivities were over, the winter grew cold and long. One day in February Angel's mother said, "I think we should have a dinner party."

Angel, who had been feeling guilty about spending so little time with Rags, was playing garage mechanic with him.

"Why?" she said. "Who would come?"

"All of our friends," said her mother. "Edna, Alyce, and Margaret, and Rudy, Rags, and you and I."

That sounded like a lot of people to Angel—and a lot of work.

"It seems time to celebrate Rudy's job," Mrs. O'Leary said.

Angel had never thought of jobs as things to celebrate. Celebrations were for birthdays or report cards or weddings or new babies. But a job was as good as anything, she supposed, and if it kept Rudy here, it was surely worth celebrating. She hated to think what would happen to Rags if he left. And her mother. Both of them might go to pieces.

"That's a good idea," said Angel.

Her mother looked pleased that Angel liked her idea.

"A party! A party!" shouted Rags. "Will there be presents? And cake?"

"Of course," said their mother.

"Games?" said Rags. "And prizes?"

"No games," said her mother. "It will be a dinner party. We'll think of some good food to have."

"I'll make the place cards," said Angel, who was already thinking of where she could get some flowers to put on them as a live decoration.

"Well, first," said Mrs. OLeary, "we have to think about invitations and find a day when everyone can come. Then we have to plan the food and shop for it."

Angel got a piece of paper and wrote down the people her mother had named. Then she thought of another person, and her mother thought of someone else, and Rags suggested Angel's teacher be invited, and before long there were twelve names on the list.

"That's enough," said their mother. "That's all we can handle. We have just enough good china to serve twelve."

"When should we have it?" said Angel. "We have to choose a day."

"I think a Sunday would be good," said her mother. "Let me call Rudy and see if a week from Sunday is a good time."

When her mother reached Rudy, he said that

a week from Sunday was a fine day, and that he would enjoy a dinner party.

"What can I bring?" Angel heard him ask.

"Just yourself," said her mother.

"Yourself! Yourself!" Rags laughed. He thought that was terribly funny.

"No," Rudy said. "I have to contribute something, too. What about some champagne? How would that be? And some pop for the children."

"Why, that would be very nice," said Mrs. O'Leary. "That will be very festive, having champagne to drink."

The next afternoon Angel and her mother went downtown to shop for invitations. There didn't seem to be any invitations to a dinner party for someone who had a new job, but finally Angel's mother found one that said, "Come help us celebrate."

"We can write in that it's a dinner party," said Mrs. O'Leary.

"And write in to bring a present," said Rags when they got home.

"Rags, you can't ask for presents," said Angel. "This isn't a birthday party, anyway."

"Mom said there'll be presents," said Rags, sulking.

"We'll buy small presents," said his mother, "for everybody, to put by their plates."

Rags seemed to be satisfied.

Angel and her mother addressed the invitations. They added the date and time and R.S.V.P., which meant that the guests should respond whether they could come or not.

Angel took the invitations to the post office and put them down the slot herself to be sure they didn't get lost.

Before long the phone was ringing, and soon they knew everyone could come except one person, who had to be out of town.

"Now," said Mrs. O'Leary, "we can plan the menu and shop for food."

"And get cards to make the place cards," said Angel.

Angel purchased the things she needed for

the place cards. While she was in the stationery store, she got some party napkins and a large party tablecloth and some noisemakers that looked as if they were for New Year's Eve but weren't.

Angel's mother got out the sterling silver serving dishes and the crystal candlesticks and the wax tapers. Everything that was silver had to be polished. Dishes that Angel had never seen appeared from the high storage cupboards and were washed. Angel began to think that a dinner party was a lot of work. Every day after school there was something more to do to get ready.

"It will be worth it," said her mother cheerfully when Angel mentioned all the work. "It isn't often we have a large dinner party."

Angel was glad about that. Especially since, as the party grew closer, her mother appeared to be getting nervous that things wouldn't all run smoothly.

"It's hard to have everything all cooked at

the same time, Angel," said Mrs. O'Leary one day as she was studying one of her cookbooks.

Angel knew cooking wasn't easy. When Alyce came by, she said, "Many hands make light work," but Angel reminded her that "too many cooks spoil the broth," and Alyce laughed uproariously, as if Angel had said something very funny.

The menu they finally decided on was "a nice juicy ham with pineapple slices and cloves on top of it," oven-browned potatoes roasted around the ham, and cauliflower supreme (that meant it had a cheese sauce over it), two mold-ed salads, hot rolls, fresh peas, and homemade apple pie with ice cream.

"I can make the salads ahead of time — Angel, you can help me — and the apple pies we'll bake in the morning. The ham and potatoes will be easy because they just go into the oven for an hour and a half, and when you take them out, they're all ready — no last-minute gravy and fussing at the stove."

As the day grew closer, Mrs. O'Leary thought of other things to add to the menu, like deviled eggs and snacks to have with the drinks. Angel and Rags helped her make everything that could possibly be frozen or refrigerated.

Angel couldn't find any wildflowers this early in the season, so she made flowers out of scraps of material instead. She printed names neatly on the cards and stood them against the water goblets after the table was set. Angel drew a little microphone and clown's face on Rudy's card instead of a flower.

The morning of the dinner party dawned bright and clear and sunny. Dinner was scheduled for six o'clock (before Rags got tired and difficult, Mrs. O'Leary said) and the people were coming at five.

Angel put on her dotted swiss party dress at three-thirty and helped Rags put on his new matching pants and T-shirt.

Rudy was the first one to arrive.

"It looks like a party, it smells like a party, it

must *be* a party!" he shouted, his arms filled with bags.

Soon the guests began to arrive, and Angel carried glasses in on trays and served snacks and appetizers on silver plates. Rags passed paper plates and small napkins with exploding stars so that the guests did not spill deviled eggs or champagne on their clothes.

"Every single thing is in the oven!" said Angel's mother at four-thirty.

"Except the ice cream!" said Rags.

Everyone tittered.

"Yes!" said their mother. "And the salad, of course!"

Angel's mother wiped her hands and went into the living room and sat down with a glass of champagne. Angel was relieved to notice that she was relaxing. This party had been getting her nerves on edge, even though she said it would be easy.

Rudy had put the phonograph on and the guests began to sing.

Now Rudy was dancing with Alyce, and Edna was dancing with Rags! Everyone seemed to be having a very good time.

Suddenly Rudy said, "Who would like to see my new studio over at the station? It's only about a five-minute walk."

The television show had turned out to be so successful that the manager had found a larger studio for Rudy and brought in new equipment.

Everyone said they would, and started trooping toward the door. "Come on, kids," he said to Angel and Rags and their mother.

"Well, I suppose everything will do just fine in the oven," said Mrs. O'Leary.

So everyone followed Rudy to the station, where he gave them a tour and showed them how a TV show was put on and even let Rags talk into the microphone and let everyone see themselves on the TV monitor in the studio.

By six o'clock everyone was back at the house, and Angel's mother said, "We can all sit down in the dining room now!"

Angel seated the guests, even though they could see where their places were from the cards, and then she served the salads as Mrs. O'Leary got them ready.

"My, this is delicious!" said Margaret Toomer. "I'll have to have the recipe!"

Everyone had opened the gifts at their plates and were having a good time comparing them. Rags got a Matchbox truck, which he was running up and down the tablecloth, in and out and around the salt and pepper shakers.

After the salad course, everyone began to use the noisemakers (led by Rags), and Angel cleared the plates.

Then, just as she sat down again to await the main course, Angel heard her mother scream. No one else seemed to hear her, with all the noise in the dining room, but Angel knew a scream when she heard it. She dashed into the kitchen.

Mrs. O'Leary had opened the oven door and had taken the cover off the roaster that held the juicy, tender ham with the pineapple and cloves and the potatoes around it. Her mother pointed. The ham was there, juicy and tender. There was only one thing wrong with it.

"It's green!" said Angel, shocked. "Why is it green?"

Her mother began to cry. Angel put her arms around her to soothe her.

"My dinner party that I planned so carefully!" she cried. "It's a failure! We can't eat a bright green ham and bright green potatoes! Whatever could have gone wrong?"

"Anything the matter?" called Rudy, sticking his head around the doorway.

Angel's mother walked over to him and threw her head onto his chest. "Our dinner is ruined," she sobbed. "I knew something would go wrong. I felt it in my bones."

Rudy walked over to the oven and looked at the roaster. He looked thoughtful. "Perhaps the meat was spoiled," he said.

"It was a fresh ham from the butcher shop,"

said Mrs. O'Leary. "It wasn't even a canned ham. The butcher said it was fresh as could be!"

"Don't panic," said Rudy. "We can think about this. Everyone is having a good time talking."

It was true. The guests did not miss the hostess. Laughter and talking and noisemakers could be heard from the dining room.

"Maybe it's just on the outside," said Rudy. "We can cut the outside off and it will be pink and tender inside!"

Rudy took a large fork and lifted the ham onto a platter. Green gravy dripped along the floor and stove and onto the platter.

Rudy carved one slice off the edge. The next slice was still green. He cut the next slice and the next one — all green.

He cut a potato with a fork. It was a solid green inside, too.

Now Angel's mother was crying in earnest. "Whatever could have caused it?" she said. "And what are we going to do?"

"I'll go out and get Chicken Smiley," said Rudy.

"Smiley's isn't open on Sunday," said Angel. "Nothing's open on Sunday."

"And we can't serve our guests take-out food at a dinner party," said her mother. "Not when we sent out invitations."

Angel and Rudy were both thinking that take-out food would be better than wieners or peanut butter and jelly sandwiches. But they didn't say it.

"If we only knew what it was," sobbed Mrs. O'Leary.

"It may not be a bit dangerous," said Rudy doubtfully.

"We can't eat it. Everyone may get sick," said Angel, "and even die."

Rudy was tasting the green gravy from the large metal spoon in the roaster. "It doesn't taste bad!" he said. "It tastes very good!" He nibbled at the ham.

"It's fine!" he said. "It's tender and juicy!"

"But what *is* it?" Mrs. O'Leary repeated.

Realizing that there was no food on his plate, Rags had come running around the comer and into the kitchen. He stared at the ham. Then he did a terrible thing. He ran to the bookcase and got his favorite Dr. Seuss book, and recited out loud:

I will not eat green eggs and ham,
I will not eat them, Sam I am.

Everyone in the dining room was listening to Rags read the book he knew by heart, and they were applauding. He then held up the book so they could see the picture of the green, green ham, not unlike the one in the kitchen.

"We've got green ham!" said Rags. "We've got green ham, Sam I am!"

Everyone laughed.

All of a sudden, as Angel looked at the large metal spoon in the green liquid and noticed the green drops along the floor and stove, she knew. It couldn't be true, but it was. The roaster was the pan that she had used to dye her sneakers. She thought she had washed it out, but dye must have clung to it and dried. It wasn't noticed because the roaster was one of those marbleized dark blue pans.

How could it be that the chartreuse dye that wouldn't dye her sneakers had instead dyed everything else it touched? It dyed the ham and potatoes just exactly the shade of green that she had wanted her shoes to be! In fact, the ham and potatoes were exactly the shade of green of the new sneakers that Rudy had bought her!

"It's my fault!" shouted Angel as she burst into tears. "It's all my fault the party is ruined! I dyed my sneakers in this pan!"

Her mother turned to her in surprise. She looked as if she wanted to scold Angel, but she just stood there with her mouth open.

Rudy threw back his head and laughed and laughed. "I knew I had seen this color somewhere. It's the color of Angel's new sneakers!"

Angel didn't know when she had been so

miserable. Well, maybe when she thought her mother was under arrest. But this felt even worse. She had wasted a perfectly good, expensive ham just by being careless.

"Tell me, Angel, do you know if this is food dye or if it is poisonous?" asked Rudy.

"It said on the envelope that is was safe. The Food and Drug Administration said that."

"All right. That's what I thought. You two go and sit down, and I'll serve the main course."

He pushed them gently out of the kitchen. Angel and her mother sat down at the table with red eyes and joined in the conversation.

In just a few minutes, Rudy appeared in the dining room bearing a large platter with the green ham neatly sliced in juicy uniform pieces. The green potatoes were arranged all around the edge of the platter in a circle. And on top of the ham slices were green slices of pineapple arranged in the shape of a shamrock! Peering out from under the potatoes was a nest of green, green parsley.

"And now," announced Rudy in his stage voice, "in celebration of St. Patrick's Day, which is not too far off, we have an Irish dinner!" Rudy began to do a sort of Irish jig as he put the platter down on the table. He was humming "The Irish Washerwoman."

"Why, how lovely!" murmured Margaret Toomer.

"What an original idea for a holiday!" said Alyce. "I'll have to find out how you did that!"

"Is it corned beef and cabbage?" said Edna, whose mother always cooked that on St. Patrick's Day.

"No!" shouted Rags. "It's green ham! Green eggs and ham. I cannot eat them Sam I am!"

Angel watched as the guests eagerly helped themselves to the lime green dinner. Sure enough, they were *eating it!* And when the food on the platter was gone, Rudy quietly went to the kitchen and refilled it.

Rudy had performed magic once again. He had turned an inedible dinner into a holiday feast!

As they ate, there were discussions of the possibilities of serving a red and green turkey for Christmas and pink pork chops on Valentine's Day.

"It would be very festive!" said Alyce.

"That was clever of your mom to make green ham," said Edna.

"It wasn't supposed to be green," whispered Angel. "Remember the pan we dyed my shoes in?"

Edna's eyes grew large. Then she covered her mouth with her hand and said, "Oh, no!"

Angel nodded.

"But your shoes were in that dye!" said Edna. "Your dirty shoes!"

"Sssh," said Angel. She had hoped Edna wouldn't think of that. It had bothered Angel when she thought that she was the only one who knew about her shoes being in the pan. But everyone enjoyed it, and no one was sick. Or dead. Perhaps what Alyce had once told her was true: What you don't know won't hurt you!

Rudy had now put a record on the phonograph — Bing Crosby singing "Danny Boy."

And when the dessert was brought in, each slice of apple pie had a sprig of mint stuck in the ice cream. Angel realized that that was a last-minute decision to show that the Irish motif had been planned and wasn't a haphazard, accidental thing! Why, if they had known about the green ham *before* dinner, they could have had green champagne and green deviled eggs! Angel thought of all the things it was possible to do to hide a mistake.

After dinner was all over, Rudy magically produced dark green crème de menthe in small glasses over ice for the adults. Everyone moved to the living room, where they sat in the soft chairs and were very comfortable. Then Rudy did something even more startling.

He stood up in the middle of the room and said, "May I have your attention, please?" When everyone looked at him, he raised his glass and said, "I'd like to make a toast!"

Angel thought it would be to his new job or his new studio or maybe even his new friends. But she was definitely not expecting the toast that followed.

"I have asked Mrs. O'Leary to marry me, and if it is all right with Angel and Rags, I would like to toast to our future!"

Although the words startled Angel, she wasn't really surprised. It seemed like the most natural thing in the world for Rudy to become a permanent part of the family.

Everyone lifted their crème de menthe in a toast, and cries of congratulations rang out. Mrs. O'Leary was crying, and even Alyce and Margaret had tears of happiness in their eyes.

Edna threw her arms around Angel and said, "You'll have a *father*, just think of that!"

Angel *had* thought of it. A few months before it would have terrified her. A clown for a father!

"Rags needs a father," said Angel.

"So do you," said Edna. "Especially a father as nice as Rudy."

Rudy put his arms around Angel and Rags. Rags was sitting on his knees and reciting: "Will you eat them with a bear? I will not eat them anywhere!" As far as Rags was concerned, he already had a father. This was no news to him.

After the last person had left, Rudy said, "I'll clean up the house. And Angel and Rags can help me."

While they worked, Rudy told them that the wedding would not be for some time. They all had to get to know each other better, and he would need full-time work. He said he wanted to get their mother a fine engagement ring, and they would need time to plan a nice wedding.

When the last dish was dried, and the last piece of leftover green ham was wrapped in foil and put in the refrigerator, Rudy kissed each one of them and went home to his room.

When the children were ready for bed, Mrs. O'Leary sat down beside Angel and said, "You know, I don't *have* to marry Rudy. If either one of you has an objection — if you think it isn't a good thing for the family—it isn't too late to change the plans."

Angel tried to picture that. Her mother saying no to Rudy and his walking out of their life. Going back to Washington forever. No letters. No jokes. No surprises and no loving Rudy. She realized their life must have been dull before he came.

"Do *you* want to marry him?" asked Angel.

"Well, yes, of course, Angel, but I don't want to do anything you and Rags wouldn't like..."

"If you're happy, we'll be happy. Besides," added Angel, "I think we all love Rudy."

"I think so, too," said her mother.

The last thing Angel heard as she turned out her light and curled up in her own warm bed was Rags making up a new chant.

A clown is never ever sad,
A clown is never very mad,
A clown is perfect for a dad.